"Any Man Who Kisses The Way You Do Has Had A Great Deal Of Experience,"

Sally said. "I feel beyond my depth."

"You're the first woman I've ever wanted."

"Pah!"

He was cooling more. "How can you be so in control when I'm a shambles? Do you go around attacking men that way just so you can see how bad the wreck will be?"

"Of course not. I've never been serious be—"

He waited. When she didn't continue, his arms tightened just a fraction. "You were experimenting? That's playing with fire. Not matches, but the real thing."

"No. I only wanted a kiss...I believe you are a roué. I think you've left a trail of devastated women behind you. You probably had to leave some town before you came here."

"No. I'm a good man."

"You kiss like a wicked one."

Dear Reader,

You know, there are some months here at Silhouette Desire that I feel are simply perfect! Naturally, I think each and every Desire book is just wonderful, but occasionally the entire lineup is so special I have to mention each book separately.

Let's start with *Hazards of the Heart* by Dixie Browning. This talented author has been writing for the line since nearly the very beginning—over ten years ago! Still, it's hard for me to believe that this is her *fiftieth* Silhouette book. *Hazards of the Heart* is highlighted as our *Man of the Month,* and it also contains a special letter from Dixie to you, her loyal readers.

Joan Johnston is fast becoming a favorite, but if you haven't yet experienced her sexy western-flavored stories, please give her a try! *The Rancher and the Runaway Bride* is the first of her new series, *Hawk's Way,* which takes place—mostly—on a Texas ranch. The stories concern the lives—and new loves—of the two Whitelaw brothers and their sassy sister.

A book from Lass Small is always a delight, and this time around we have *A Disruptive Influence.* What—or *who?*— is this disruptive influence? Why, read and find out.

As far as I'm concerned, Nancy Martin has been too long from the list, therefore I'm *thrilled* with *Good Golly, Miss Molly.* Doreen Owens Malek is another author we just don't see enough of, so I'm equally excited about *The Harder They Fall.* And I love Lucy Gordon's emotional writing style. If you're also a fan, don't miss *Married in Haste.*

Six spectacular books by six dynamite authors. Can you ask for anything more?

Until next month, happy reading!

Lucia Macro
Senior Editor

LASS SMALL
A DISRUPTIVE INFLUENCE

SILHOUETTE *Desire*®

Published by Silhouette Books New York

America's Publisher of Contemporary Romance

SILHOUETTE BOOKS
300 East 42nd St., New York, N.Y. 10017

A DISRUPTIVE INFLUENCE

Copyright © 1993 by Lass Small

All rights reserved. Except for use in any review, the reproduction or utilization of this work in whole or in part in any form by any electronic, mechanical or other means, now known or hereafter invented, including xerography, photocopying and recording, or in any information storage or retrieval system, is forbidden without the permission of the publisher, Silhouette Books, 300 E. 42nd St., New York, N.Y. 10017

ISBN: 0-373-05775-X

First Silhouette Books printing April 1993

All the characters in this book have no existence outside the imagination of the author and have no relation whatsoever to anyone bearing the same name or names. They are not even distantly inspired by any individual known or unknown to the author, and all incidents are pure invention.

® and ™:Trademarks used with authorization. Trademarks indicated with ® are registered in the United States Patent and Trademark Office, the Canada Trade Mark Office and in other countries.

Printed in the U.S.A.

Books by Lass Small

LASS SMALL

finds living on this planet at this time a fascinating experience. People are amazing. She thinks that to be a teller of tales of people, places and things is absolutely marvelous.

To our nephew Bill Small
and his Heavy Weather band of Austin, TEXAS

One

In Fort Wayne, Indiana, at the Grand Wayne Center, the new vice president of marketing was observing the display section that would be occupied by his company. He surveyed the area and saw her.

One block of the exhibits was all Jamisons. The woman's booth was one of the block. She was a Jamisons employee?

She was so—busy! That was what caught Mitchell Goalong's attention. While Mitch slouched his good, hard, lean body with one hip against Pike's counter, he was listening to what Pike was saying to him, but Mitch was watching her.

He thought she was really rather average in everything: height, figure, face. She could probably spare a couple of pounds. If she was wearing really high heels, the top of her head would come up to his eyebrow.

Her hair was to her shoulders and it was the medium brown that's so common. She wore it loose and it apparently had a natural curl. Her figure was nice: good legs and a very nice bottom. Just right. An average American girl. Uh, woman.

She didn't "fuss" with the exhibit. She moved back to judge before she improved it. Then she backed off to look at it as she stood still and concentrated.

It was then that Mitch found he wasn't as interested in what she was doing as he was interested in her. She sure was female. Or was she?

She wasn't at all conscious of herself. She wasn't moving for effect as most women either do with calculation or from natural instinct.

Her quick movements, her chewed lipstick, her hair being mussed, were all witness to the fact that the woman he watched was more concerned with the display than with herself. She looked like she'd been rolled around a little, maybe on the floor.

Mitch indicated her with his chin as he asked Pike, "Who is she?"

"I can't believe you don't know."

"Well?" Mitch's impatience made him glance at Pike.

Shorter, plump and about the same age, Pike sighed. "She's the naked woman in all our lascivious dreams and in some of the scary ones, too. She's the one." Pike said that in a candid admission, as if the words were explanation enough.

Mitch gave a very patient sigh. "She's an employee and she's been with us . . . how long?"

"Six months. Would you like the exact day count? She drives us all crazy. We call her B.B. because she's such a busy bee. She interferes with everything and tells us how to handle things. She's so earnest and sincere that we all listen. That's because of the dreams we have about her. We pretend we're really listening in a businesslike way, but we're actually just watching her mouth and her gestures and how her body moves and how her eyes look at us, and we don't hear much of anything.''

Mitch waited. Pike would eventually get to the point, but in the meantime Mitch could watch that Busy Bee, partway down the aisle adjusting her display.

It was samples from the women's wear department at the Jamisons stores. The public show-off weekend called WE ARE HERE displays were being set up in the center the coming June weekend. It was to brag on what was available at the locally owned stores.

Mitch pried his stare from the woman's busy form and looked at the display. She was doing a good job. The limited space allotted to her wasn't crowded. A viewer's single glance would cover it, but their attention would then be caught. The female mannequin was buffeted by the pretend autumn wind. One hand held her hat against her head. Her suit jacket and skirt were being blown and a peek of her purple garter-belt clasp showed the top of her stocking. One knee was bent and her foot was lifted to show her shoe.

That was clever.

Mitch listened as Pike went on about the male re-action—and he remembered her name was Sally Yoder and she was twenty-seven.

She had put a very small electric fan behind several flat sheets of crafted paper. She turned the fan on and that gentle breeze tumbled some anchored leaflike autumn-colored papers. It was visually eye-catching and the viewers' attention would be drawn down to the model's flipping skirt. Excellent.

Sally studied the effect and then turned off the fan to reset it more precisely. She tested it again.

"—and the problem is, that she is ALWAYS right! That's the thing that makes us all step back and hesitate."

Mitch's green eyes slitted. So she was always right? As zonked as they were about her, she intimidated them? They had all stepped back from her and hesitated? Mitch's nice chiseled lips curved in a tomcat's prowling smile.

The double B's shirt had pulled loose from her skirt. She wore track shoes. There was a pencil stuck into her hair, behind her ear. She never glanced up. She was so concentrated on her display that she didn't know anyone else was anywhere around.

Mitch looked at the other setups. They were adequately done. Nice. Professional. Standard.

He looked back at Sally's. While the other displays were inanimate, hers moved and drew the eye. She was putting labels on different parts of the model. Mitch judged the labels would be clear to someone stopping and looking at them, but the labels weren't at all intrusive to the overall scene.

Since he wondered what the labels said, so would anyone else.

Pike was saying, "...and she pulled her hand back and swatted him alongside his head. But he didn't get mad! She told him, 'Don't you ever do that again! Do you hear me?' She treated him just like she was grownup and he was a budding Lothario who was all testosterone and not much sense. The guys all hooted and laughed, and he just shook his head, but he had to grin, too. He'd really been clumsy and he knew—''

"Who was that?" Mitch's glance suddenly rested on Pike.

"Haven't you been listening? It was Andy. He watches her now with his heart in his mouth, just like all the rest of us. We can do that because she never notices us unless we do something for her. Then she smiles like an angel and is so pleased. We're busting our butts trying to get her okay. Do you know what it cost me, in hours traded, to get this spot where I can see her? You'd be sick to your stomach if you knew."

Then Mitch's narrowed green eyes slid around and he noticed the booths overlooking hers. Not one male was doing a thing. They were watching that busy/busy figure of Sally Yoder. Even Jake was watching, and he was old enough to be her grandfather.

Mitch decided that after the exhibition he'd recommend the Jamisons fire the distraction. His slitted gaze rested on her again. Well. He had enough contacts that he could help her find another place. Then he considered the contacts and eliminated a few.

Mitchell was almost six feet tall and he was rapidly approaching thirty, that division between youth and maturity. His hair was the average brown of Sally's. He wore clothes like a model and was just as nice looking in sweats. He knew he looked good. But he was brought up by foster parents who had reminded him that he needed more than looks to make it in the world.

He'd found the way he looked came in handy in some cases and was a liability in others. He knew it was the same for women at any age.

His monitoring glances kept going back to the Busy Bee, but he did keep one ear listening casually to Pike, not discouraging his long commentary on *the* Sally Yoder.

She stepped back. Then she walked away. Panic touched in Mitch and he was disgusted with himself. She would be back. Just then she turned and did exactly that. She walked along, looking at the various displays, rather absently nodding at the greetings given her, and she walked by her own display, glancing at it.

She walked on past before she returned, strolling, looking aside to the other exhibits, smiling automatically or lifting a hand, but her focus was on her own exhibit. She passed it a second time.

She went back and adjusted the fan again. And she repeated her critical pass-bys.

She was fascinating.

She stood and stared. Then she left.

She simply... left.

The feeling of the day became overcast. The intent people in the surrounding booths began to stir aimlessly and talk idly.

Mitch frowned. She had been their focus. She left, and they were released from her. And Mitch noted the sobering fact that he, too, had moved and was then standing flat-footed, his big hands in his trouser pockets and his full attention was finally on Pike who was watching off to where Sally had disappeared.

She was a distraction. For the sake of efficiency, the Jamisons needed to get rid of her.

When Mitch had taken a refresher course in management last year, this very thing had been touched on. A really good-looking man or woman could wreak havoc in any organization. The man less so. His problem could be handled. But unless the female was the corporate head...or the mistress of the corporate head...she should be transferred to some remote place where she couldn't cause any turmoil. Or she should be fired using some reason good enough that the company wouldn't be sued for discrimination.

Sally's days were numbered. She had to have a usable flaw.

Although Mitch hung around for some long time appearing interested and occupied, Sally did not return.

He'd examined most of the other companies' presentations. They had done this kind of thing before because they kept their displays simple.

He finally ran out of all possible delays and he had to leave. He found he was reluctant to give up the vigil.

That thought did give him pause, because it made it appear that he was also entranced with that Busy Bee. But he searched his soul and found he was pure. He was not enticed.

He would share in the buffet lunch with the others involved at the Center. It was his right to be there, but it still pleased him when Mr. Jamison had called personally to be sure Mitch would attend.

Mitch was the man who was going to pull the Jamisons' One-Stop stores from the doldrums in which sales had stagnated.

Mitch had suggested the exhibition first to Mr. Jamison. All locally owned stores would be represented. Jamisons would be the only clothing and household store. Mitch had carried Mr. Jamison's blessings to the Chamber of Commerce, and they had organized the exhibition.

The response from other stores had been excellent and the publicity had been quite good.

They were having the Heavy Weather blues group from Austin, Texas, to play the next night, on Saturday. And that had been a big drawing card. Tickets had been sold in all the record shops and places where records were sold. They had a sellout.

Bill Small's group had arrived from Texas the night before and that day they had visited several of the Magnet schools and the three hospitals.

Media coverage had been exceptional.

Most of the Jamisons personnel who had worked on the booths were at the luncheon, and Sally was there. Mitch was circumspect. He didn't immediately go right over. He took some pictures of the top brass, who laughed and were the way people are when they want their pictures taken but aren't quite comfortable posing for them.

Jamisons higher echelon always dressed in gray suits during the day and navy suits or black formal wear in the evening. It wasn't easy to tell one Jamison from another except for the patriarch, Edgar. The Jamisons were a male family. Only one Jamison female had been produced. Her name was Abigail.

Mitch wore a navy suit and was interviewed by one of the TV reporters. He was a little surprised. Mr. Jamison lifted a glass of iced tea and nodded from across the room. He'd set it up.

Mitch had taken a class in interviews and how to handle those scheduled and especially those unscheduled.

The woman interviewing asked, "Why did you think this would be successful?"

A nice leading question. "We have great locally owned and operated stores right here in Fort Wayne. We wanted the citizens to be reminded of that. This is a good city. We're proud to be a part of it."

So she asked, "Are you a native?"

Ah, yes. He grinned. "A recent native."

She was pleased with his reply and laughed.

And he managed to get in, "Most of those working at our stores are from this area. The shoppers will find relatives and friends at Jamisons. It's a good place. A family place."

"And you've brought in Heavy Weather from Austin, Texas."

"Yes. Like our own, it's a celebration of originality and talent."

"Who, here now, are native to the area?"

"You know the Jamison family."

The camera turned to them and they again lifted their ice-tea glasses and smiled from across the room.

"Who else?"

And he named some of the others, pointing them out. That brought Mitch to one who was also a native. The Busy Bee. "And Miss Yoder."

The cameraman appeared to have no trouble finding Miss Yoder. The camera lingered on her. She glanced up and then went on eating from the plate she carried. The cameraman was fascinated. Off to one side, Mitch recognized Pike's amused chuckle. Every man there was empathetic with the cameraman.

And Mitch *knew* every damned male there was instantly plotting a way to get home and set his VCR to tape the news that evening. Then they'd have Sally real and in living color on a tape to play over and over and over until that section of tape was ruined. And they'd play it slowly so that they could watch her mouth take the food from her fork. And she'd look up at the camera and smile, and they'd pretend that she smiled just to them. Each one would dream that.

Mitch took a calming breath and decided he'd been working rather hard on coordinating and planning the Jamisons booth choices for this exhibition. He might be a little stressed and hallucinating. And he would probably be better off if he went to his apartment, showered, shaved and changed his clothing. And set the VCR.

It was a little diminishing to realize he was no different from the rest of the ravening mob.

Well, he might find something on the tape that would help in her firing. There was always that.

He straightened up and felt more businesslike.

Then the interviewer caught the cameraman's attention and she asked Mitch, "How do you like our city?"

He blinked and smiled just a little. She was using this interview to come on to him? He replied in a kind, ordinary-guy voice, "It's home."

She shook his hand and left her card on his palm.

She and the cameraman left. Mitch watched the cameraman. He was so blasé. But Mitch narrowed his green eyes and continued to watch. Sure enough, just before he went out the door, the cameraman looked back at Sally.

Mitch immediately snapped his head around and looked at her. Her back was turned. She was getting something else from the buffet table.

Because she didn't watch after that attractive cameraman, something inside Mitch's soul was satisfied.

He worked his way over toward her with seeming happenstance. And he even contrived to bump into her. His hands were free, so he could use them to steady her. He did that quite cleverly.

She looked up and said, ''You're Mitch Goalong. I love your last name.''

And he said a practiced tried-and-true, ''Aw, go along with you.''

She tilted her head back and laughed, her blue eyes on his green ones were dancing with amusement.

And everything slowed down. People moved more slowly, and words were slowed. It was like an old ''Star Trek'' segment when Captain Kirk and Dr. Spock were trying to solve some buzzing and finally their metabolic rates were sped up as everyone else's slowed down. As Spock said then, ''It was fascinating.''

So, on an island of sanity, slowly and with all the time in the universe, there they were. He and the problem named Sally Yoder. Mitch looked at her and was, indeed, fascinated.

She licked her lips in a normal manner, but to Mitch it was slow and sensual. Soon he would be going home to his new apartment just over a couple of streets in the downtown area, and he was going to set his VCR.

She said, ''I congratulate you on being a new native.''

''It's been relatively painless.''

''Your word choice is excellent.''

''Painless?''

'' 'Relatively.' Do you have relatives in town?''

''I have a foster brother here, and I've adopted Pike as a cousin,'' he offered.

"Pike's so funny. He writes songs. Be careful for the Heavy Weather people—Pike might try to con them into trying some of his songs."

"Pike writes weird songs."

"They're country-western. And Heavy Weather could use some as blues. Have you ever read the country-western list of the best of the worst titles?"

And Mitch laughed. He realized his and Sally's metabolism had sped up and they were in synch with the rest of the people.

He hadn't progressed beyond Sally in his circuit, and he discovered other men were now gathered around her and intruding with comments and song titles from that best-of-worst list.

A laughing Sally accepted the chatter. But Mitch felt hostile to the intruders.

That was what caused him to consider his reaction to her, so he said to Sally, "I'll see you later."

In a distracted manner, she replied, "Yes," but she only glanced his way very briefly.

He left the Grand Wayne Center and walked the two blocks over to Mid-Town Crossing. Old buildings had been gutted, reconstructed and refurbished into blocks of apartments. Some were rented, some bought as condos. All were elegant. It had been a part of the reclaiming of the downtown area.

Mitch unlocked the entrance and took the stairs to his floor. There were only four apartments off that hallway. His was across the way and looked down onto South Harrison Street. He had a living room, dining room and kitchen, with two bedrooms and two baths.

He immediately programmed the VCR to tape the evening news.

The apartment was furnished with castoffs from the attics of his various family connections in Ohio. Most of the pieces had some kind of family history, some were pieces rescued from oblivion and some of the pieces were quite good. The wide bed was new.

He opened his closet to take out his clothes. He was glad that night's event was a formal affair and that he owned his own tuxedo. He took two linen handkerchiefs from his drawer and clean underwear. He put a condom in the breast pocket.

He considered. Then he realized that his foolish and shocking subconscious was hopelessly hopeful. He removed the condom and put the handkerchief in perfectly, after four tries.

How much had he and Sally spoken? Several sentences. That wasn't even the beginning of a basis for an affair. He narrowed his eyes. She probably wasn't the affair type. Her type would want commitment. He wasn't in the market for anything like that.

Showering, he decided that he would shun her. He would find the means to get her fired and he'd get over her. Get over her? What was there to "get over" with her? Nothing was started.

Mitch shaved, not seeing his own face, and he was so bemused and slow that he didn't cut himself.

He dressed with great care. He decided his carefulness was because this exhibition was important to the Jamisons and he wanted them to be comfortable with him in this new position. They would find he was not only qualified for his position, but he was a fine man who had a great future.

...Sally would stand and gaze at him with great big impressed eyes. And Mr. Jamison would slap him on his shoulder and tell him to get that girl out of there and take care of her.

His mind might be slipping.

As he checked the apartment to be sure he hadn't forgotten anything, he dutifully turned everything off, except the VCR, which he made sure was still set correctly.

He checked the money in his slim evening wallet, his handkerchiefs, change and his keys. He looked at himself in the mirror. He would do.

Taking along his small, remarkable camera, he went out his door, closing and locking it. He went down the steps to the front door, which automatically locked with any closing. Then he walked over to the Grand Wayne Center.

The exhibition opened on that Friday night with a great splash. The TV news crews and reporters from the local newspapers were present. There was a nice hoopla. Everyone was dressed up and the women were sparkly.

Mitch worked his way to where he knew Sally would be. He had a camera and he would manage to take some pictures of her. He would catch her doing something outrageous.

Now, what could she possibly do in that pack of displays and crush of people?

He didn't know of anything. He just wanted a couple of good pictures of her.

It wasn't too great a surprise to find that the Jamisons aisle leading to her exhibit was clogged with a crush of visitors. Other people were stretching up and looking and there was laughter and exclamations.

Mitch couldn't hear exactly what was causing all the to-do, but he suspected it was that woman, Sally Yoder.

And he was right.

Being almost six feet tall, he could see beyond most of the crowd of onlookers and he saw that her booth was the center of the agitation. Camera crews from the local stations were asking for assistance. "Could we have just a little room, please?"

And people were shifting all of several inches.

Then someone found chairs and other camera persons were up on chairs and asking those in front to please step aside for just a minute?

And Mitch narrowed his eyes. She had done something newsworthy. That could well be the basis for his getting her fired. There hadn't been anything in that booth that afternoon that would now cause the newspeople to be so interested.

The pitch of amusement and animated chatter continued among those involved in the actual scene.

Once Mitch heard her voice saying, "It is true. Have you ever had it happen to you?"

Her voice was logical and precise. It was...businesslike. Under the circumstances, that was strange.

The responding laughter after her words was so amused.

What had she done? He had to know.

"Pardon me," he said to the person in front of him.

The man didn't even look around. He just said, "No."

Never in Mitch's life had anyone replied to such a request with a negative. What was the world coming to?

More firmly, he said, "Move it." And his voice wasn't at all nice.

"Up yours."

"I'm security."

"Let's see your ID."

Just think of the guts of the ordinary citizen. It was probably subliminal reaction to the failure of the S & L's, the closing of Grissom Air Base, the monetary carelessness of politicians.

Mitch flashed a quick peek of a library card laid over his driver's license.

"What's that for?"

"Undercover."

"Jeeeezzzz, you guys are everywhere."

"Yes."

The blocker shifted three inches in a not-very-courteous manner.

Mitch progressed slowly. He was aware of the brilliant lighting ahead for the cameras held high. He used his library card/driver's license with fair success until some guy growled, "Who you think you're kidding?"

So Mitch was stopped there. He raised up on tiptoe and stretched his neck. He could see that Busy Bee being very cool.

While she did smile, she treated the amusing incident as no big deal. As logical.

The question was urgent: WHAT was so logical that it would cause such attraction? Logic was never attractive to the media. While sin was, so were mistakes, murder and mayhem. Logic was not newsworthy.

Mitch began to feel restless and a bit perturbed. The Jamisons Company was rather formal and anything that caused all this attention had to be one of the newsworthy items. It wasn't murder or mayhem. People were amused. It was a mistake or a sin.

And Mitch wondered how he was going to counter whatever that witch had contrived in order for him to save the company's reputation.

"The World News Network will love this!"

That had been one of the cameramen.

And *she* said, "Get our name and city correct."

That *is* what she said!

Mitch's teeth clamped together and his jaw muscles were rigid. His breath picked up and his body tensed.

The news teams began backing or pushing their way out of the growing throng, saying, "Sorry. We have a deadline. Let us through. Please. Sorry. Oops. Thanks."

Mitch didn't move an inch. He wasn't sure if he should allow the cameras to leave. There was the great possibility that he should confiscate them all and smash them. He had a gut feeling a disaster was looming.

With the leaking away of people from the solid mass, Mitch gradually could see Sally Yoder clearer.

She was serene. She was in a spangly evening dress with narrow shoulder straps. She looked beautiful. She sparkled. Her eyes were alive and well made up without seeming so. Her hair was a volume that framed her face.

Pike's booth was nearby. Pike got down from a chair as the crowd eased and he saw Mitch. "Can you beat it? She always does something that rocks everybody!" And he laughed.

Mitch cleared his throat and made his voice normal. It came out rather deadly. "What did who do?"

"That could be the title of a great song! I'll write it down."

"Pike!"

"Yeah, Mitch?"

"What did the Yoder woman do?"

Pike laughed. "Wait until you see. You have to give that girl credit. We'll be on every newscast in the country."

And Mitch could only think: My God, what has she done?

While Mitch had thought he was planted solid, he found he was being shoved along as others came behind him and were straining to see what had caused all the fuss.

Gradually he was pushed forward and he had no choice. He came to her display. He looked. It seemed the same. The labels were excellent.

The one on the model's hair said, "Our wigs don't blow away." And the one on the suit said, "Our suits keep their crease and look fresh all day." And the one on the model's face said, "Our makeup lasts." The one on the hat said, "Our hats can blow off."

And someone pointed.

Around the model's ankle was a fallen brief piece of silk. The tag on it said, "Our panties don't come off by accident."

Two

A man of almost thirty isn't that far from being nineteen, and Mitch was amused. A laugh shivered inside all of his bones and he was hard put to keep a sober face. In the press of people who exclaimed and laughed, his face was stern but his eyes danced with humor.

Sally saw that.

But his voice was stern. "Miss Yoder, you should have gotten clearance."

"Why?"

"Cooler heads might have prevailed."

She had to lean forward so that they could hear one another over the sounds of feet shuffling and laughing comments. She said with some backbone, "We're on the news. If something horrific doesn't happen, we'll make World News Network."

As a competent adult, he explained rather kindly, "That isn't publicity, that's notoriety. And—" he made it a lecture ""—notoriety is to be shunned."

She selected the word. "Shunned." She gave him a very patient look.

"You appear to be a modest woman. I am shocked you'd choose this method of calling attention to yourself."

She spaced the words with the kindness shown a half-wit for whom there could be little hope. "I am a bystander. My panties are—"

He looked down her body with some avid quickness.

"—on. It is that inanimate model who has lost the panties, not I. But obviously you've never lost a pair in public."

He was appalled. "You have? *How?* What happened?"

"I wore some that buttoned. They were French silk and very elegant. I wore them to church the first time I wore a fur coat and I walked elegantly up the stairs and my panties slid right down, almost tripping me, and I was some...discomforted." She gave him a prim flick of a glance.

With his avid curiosity concentrated on her in the pressing, noisy crowd, he asked, "What did you do?"

"I cleverly stepped from them, put them in my coat pocket and went on inside as if I had no knowledge of the incident. And all during service I scolded my guardian angel. That was my basic research for this portion of the exhibit. That is the salacious, rash pair from that impressionable time." She looked at him and tidied up her account. "Since they wear pants, men never lose their drawers."

He understood that.

"I have no reason to stay, my exhibit explains itself. Will you excuse me or do you want to scold and irritate me some more?"

He'd...irritated her. He frowned and took her hand as he turned and plowed his way through the crowd. She followed and didn't snatch her hand from his. He was especially conscious of that. The guys thought she was untouchable?

Several times they were stymied by stretching bodies who wanted to see the exhibit that was causing all the attraction. Squashed together, he could feel her against his back. He wanted to turn and hold her against his front.

And he understood his feelings existed because he wanted to protect her from the crush of the crowd. Of course. That was understandable. It was because he knew how clever men apologetically took advantage of women...in crowds.

Then he bit his lip and found he was concentrating on how he was going to explain this rhubarb to the Jamisons.

Why should he? It was the perfect out. He could just tell this little B.B. that she wasn't quite right for a town like Fort Wayne, and that she might try Chicago or New York because everyone knew just about anything goes in those places. Then, of course, there was always California which was totally wild, and it was going to break off any minute and drift out to sea, anyway.

He didn't want her to go to California.

As they emerged from the edge of the packed aisle, Mitch caught a glimpse of the Jamisons. They were grave faced and very serious. One looked sternly at

Mitch and then saw whom he towed. That Jamison spoke to the others and they moved away purposefully. But they nodded to Mitch as if to congratulate him for getting the culprit in hand.

Instead of being pleased, Mitch found he was unsettled. The disapproval was obvious in that one glance. That they moved away to avoid Sally was even worse.

Worse? Her firing would now be simple. But he would have to caution the Jamisons about gender discrimination. They wouldn't want to be sued. Firing a female was dangerous.

Well, of course, if the culprit was *male,* like Mitchell Goalong, they would have no trouble getting rid of him. He had no rights.

So... if he should take up the cause of the albatross now hanging around the Jamisons' necks, he was laying himself open to being an unsuitable employee.

It was an interesting thought.

Unconsciously, he took a better grip on Sally's hand. When she wiggled her fingers to be released, indicating that she had other things to do, he said over his shoulder to her, "Don't."

Without speaking further, he looked at her very seriously. She gave him the same regard. With her in tow, he went to look up the seating arrangement for the formal dinner... which the public had been invited to attend as paying guests.

Tables were being shifted so that more could be added.

It had been Mitch's suggestion that each round table have a representative from one of the exhibiting businesses. He asked the harried person in charge of seating where Miss Yoder was to sit.

They found her readily enough. Mitch moved her next to him at his table. Arbitrarily. He suggested several people to replace Miss Yoder at her table. He gave no reason. He just did it.

She stood, silently thoughtful through all that and offered no comment.

When the transaction was completed and the name cards changed, Mitch looked at Miss Yoder. She returned his look. Neither made any comment.

When Sally wanted to freshen her makeup, Mitch accompanied her to the ladies' door and he went to the men's room. While there, who hurried in but Edgar Jamison?

Standing alongside Mitch, Mr. Jamison said, "My boy, you've done brilliantly. You're worth your weight. You've defanged that notorious woman. Keeping her with you is brilliant. I can depend on you." He beamed.

Quite confidently and very clearly, Mitch replied, "There is no problem. We'll discuss all this on Monday."

"Right." Mr. Jamison nodded, his smile wider. "You are amazing!" And he zipped up and left happily.

So Mitch's selfishness in herding Miss Yoder so that she was exclusively in his company had been mistaken as control of an appalling situation? Mitch frowned. The Jamisons considered Sally a "situation" with which Mitch was dealing. As if she were some child who'd made a social gaffe, was too old to be dismissed from the room but had to be monitored.

He waited for her to emerge from the ladies' room. He needed to monitor her? He looked down her body. He could handle that.

They moved around the exhibits and none compared to Sally's. All the others were well done and as they were expected to appear. Sally's exhibit was the attention getter.

Mitch mentioned in a friendly manner. "My zipper stuck once."

"Who helped you?"

"I was fourteen, in middle school, and an old biddy about thirty-five had to help me."

"Thirty-five." She said only the age in a normal way.

"Something wrong with my thinking a woman over twice my age was old?"

"I suppose not."

"You're twenty-seven."

"Now, how did you know that? You looked me up?"

He slid a look down to her mouth. "I counted your rings." Like on a tree.

She laughed.

"How do you like working at Jamisons?"

"They're a little staid."

So she did recognize that. He wouldn't have to warn her anymore about their reaction to her rash conduct. "Do you always wave a red flag to see what sort of reaction you might get?"

"It depends on whether I'm willing to dodge."

He gave her a surprised look. "You just stand there and deliberately rock the boat?"

She shrugged. "That's progress."

"That's getting fired."

"There are other places."

She might not sue.

A local band, The Hush, was playing rock, feet moved and some went to the floor to dance. Mitch asked Sally, "Do you dance?"

"Yes."

But she didn't move. He gave her an almost smile. "Would you dance with me?"

"Can you?"

"Of course."

"You don't look the type."

He began to lead her to the floor. "What is the look of the 'type'?"

"A little looser."

"Are you being sassy?"

"Probably."

They moved into the wiggling, moving people and found a place. He surprised her. She laughed out loud but the sound was muffled in the noise of people talking and the band's good music.

He was discreet, indicating clearly that he could be more free and was controlling himself enough. He smiled and licked his lips and led her in coordinated steps.

The band played a couple of couple-dancing pieces, and he handled that with great skill, leading her beautifully and showing her off.

"How did you learn to dance that way?" She watched his guiding of her steps.

"Earnest teachers."

And even that amused her. "Where is your hometown?"

"Temple, Ohio. Your next question will be, where's that? I'll reply, below Cleveland and on the Cuyahoga River. You're readily familiar with the town and that river?" He turned her, watching to see that she had the room on the floor to make the turn comfortably.

"Actually...no."

"You have heard of Cleveland?"

"I believe so."

"And you heard about the Cuyahoga River burning?"

"The...river...burned?"

"Yep. The fire department had to put it out."

"Flood debris?"

"Some. Most was pollution and junk."

"Why. That's terrible."

"That was years ago. It's pristine now."

"Things can be cleaned up. See? It was done and everyone accepts that, instead of continuing to celebrate that fact."

"You would be amazed by the people who vividly remember watching the river's fire being extinguished laboriously by the red-faced Cleveland fire department...on World News Network."

She laughed. "So you were born and raised in Temple, Ohio?"

"Not exactly. I was a half orphan. My mother was still living. She was unable to respond or care for herself. She wasn't on any life support, but she lived. I grew up in the Browns' household in Temple. They've spent their lives involved in all kinds of things. One of those was that they took in stray kids. I was one. They've treated me like family. As I've mentioned, I have a foster brother here in Fort Wayne. He's Rod Brown. He has an auto shop and he's an exhibitor here at the center. That's his exhibit over there. He was married in Temple last Christmas to a Fort Wayne lady, Pat Ullick."

"Why, I know her! She does volunteer work at Lutheran Hospital. Your brother is a lucky, lucky man."

"I believe that. But he knows it."

"That's really nice."

The music had paused and they stood looking at each other. He offered, "Rod and Pat just acquired two little boys my foster dad, Salty, found for them, and Pat's pregnant. Rod feels his cup is running over."

"That must be wonderful."

"You'll have to meet them."

"I already know Pat. I'd heard she was married. She'll be a perfect mother. She almost adopted two little kids she'd been helping with. But you would know about that."

"Yeah."

"It was really tough that she had to let them go, but now she'll have three this year! Three in a lump might be a little much."

"Rod was the eldest of us all and he's had a lot of experience with kids of all ages. Pat's no novice. As you know, she's been a volunteer, helping with other people's kids for a long time, so they're handling it just fine." He smiled as he glanced around before he added, "They're really cute, those two little boys. They think Rod's some kind of a god."

He moved Sally so that a marauding intruder would be foiled, and he said, "Sorry, fella." Then he said to Sally, "The buffet's open, would you like to get something to eat?"

"All right." She was rather charmed and only a little irritated that Mitch should be controlling her access to other men. She would see if she would tolerate that.

There were multiple lines around the attractive food-laden tables. It didn't take long to be served. They carried their plates to their own table and found only one vacant chair. No one was paying any attention to name cards.

They sought a table. Actually, Mitch found places at a table on the shadowed edge. No one was seated there, so Mitch led Sally to a chair that placed her back to the ballroom floor. He figured no one would notice.

She drew men like a honeybee.

The problem was that most of the intruders weren't Jamisons men. They were strangers. That way, they didn't realize how intrusive they were being. Mitch tried to shut them out, but Sally was courteous. There's nothing worse than a well-bred woman who is courteous so that people don't feel awkward.

She said, "No," when one man asked if the chair next to her was taken.

She agreed with a man across the table that the food was nicely served.

She agreed with that first man, next to her, that she wasn't Wendall Mandell, the name on the card at her place. After the bold and intrusive male gave her his card, she introduced him to Mitch.

But she hadn't given her own name.

It wasn't much to give him heart, but Mitch was comforted that she wasn't really a flirt or a hunting woman. Not too obviously. After all, she *was* twenty-seven.

He said that to her. "You're very discreet among all these single men. You act aloof. Even though you're still single and you're already twenty-seven."

She turned her shoulder to him and talked to everyone else at the table.

She ignored his attempts to get a word in edgewise and she excused herself and left the table.

He didn't see her again that night.

He wasn't too long in figuring out that maybe she was sensitive about not being married. Then about three the next morning an odd thought occurred to him. It was possible that she deliberately was not married.

Was he out of step with the world? He'd known women had gone through a long delay about marriage and children, but that was changing. Prominent women have been open about wanting to have a baby. There was the now worn-out quote about their biological clocks ticking away.

Mitch thought that either he was a throwback or Sally was. Maybe . . . just maybe she had no interest in marriage?

He really thought that would be too bad. She was really a very nice person. A little too bold in her conduct, but actually she was pretty nice.

He went to sleep with that thought. His dreams were of his trying to capture her attention long enough in a crush of men so that he could encourage her to think well of herself.

Saturday's open house at the Grand Wayne Center was very nicely successful. Some people just came because they had a connection with the owners of the stores whose wares were on display. But some had seen the televised report on the news and they came because of Sally's well-done exhibit. They were charmed by her.

She handed out coupons for discounts and she laughed with women who shared the fact that they had lost or almost lost their underwear or knew someone who had.

Mitch saw that no one had removed that garment from the model's foot.

He roved and roamed and passed Sally's display too many times. He found her with no one there and blurted, "Have lunch with me?"

She blinked once and said, "All right."

Not aware of how abrupt his invitation had been, he found he was critical of her only agreeing reply.

He fooled her. He took her to his apartment.

She glanced around at his rooms and looked out of his windows. "I'm so glad to see inside one of these apartments. I've watched them being done, but I've never had the opportunity to see inside. They've had open houses, but they were always at the wrong time. This is very, very nice."

"The people are all pleasant. I've been in the other apartments in this wing for drinks or coffee."

She nodded. She wasn't the least bit awkward being in his isolated apartment. She didn't think of herself as vulnerable. He was somewhat irked. How many guys' apartments had she been in?

He'd laid in picnic things and he had an actual picnic basket that had come from an elderly aunt's estate. He put in cloth napkins and a card-table cloth on top of the food.

They carried the basket the few blocks over to Freimann Square by the unusually designed Civic Theatre. Their widened view of the park included that strange tumble of huge Tinkertoy-type appendages oddly labeled as sculpture.

He asked her, "Do you have plans for the Fourth? We could come here for a late supper and watch the fireworks from here."

"Well, I do have plans. Will you be by yourself?"

"I'm not sure. As you know, I'm fairly new here." He glanced to see if that affected her at all. But she knew his brother Rod was in town. Too bad he'd mentioned that. She wouldn't feel responsible for him being alone during a holiday.

She appeared relaxed and very comfortable. She didn't feel the need to entertain him. She was silent, watching the water spout from the fountains in the nicely calculated pools.

He looked around. There weren't too many people there. With the thickening trees, it was somewhat isolated. He looked at her to see if she was uneasy.

And just then two cops came walking through.

He said, "I guess we should be getting back."

She smiled. "This was a treat."

One of the cops came over and said, "Hi, Sally."

"Well, hi, Ben. How's it going?"

"Not good enough. What are you up to?"

"Jamisons is part of the exhibition over at the Wayne Center. I'm helping."

"That's where the Heavy Weather group plays tonight?"

"Right."

"Keep an eye out for me. I'd like a dance."

"I'll save you one."

And the other cop said, "Me, too."

She scoffed, "Yeah, George, and Sue will want to share."

"You're such a nasty stickler!"

The two men laughed and walked away. Mitch watched them go. They hadn't even looked at him.

As the two cops went out of sight, Mitch asked, "Will you save me some dances tonight?"

She glanced over at him. "All right."

"You're a very good dancer."

"Thank you."

"Do you suppose the time will come when we'll finally be comfortable together?"

"Perhaps."

That didn't sound encouraging. But she had come away from the center for lunch just with him. She could have vanished again as she had last night. "Where did you go last night? You disappeared."

"It had been a long day. I went home."

He'd looked up her address. She lived northeast of town.

She said, "We need to get back."

"Are you planning on leaving those panties on the model's ankle tonight?"

"Yes."

Her reply wasn't at all tentative.

Having packed up his basket, they carried the things back to his apartment. She helped him to straighten up and discard and put the dishes into the dishwasher.

At the Grand Wayne Center the afternoon was well attended, but those who passed slowly along, looking, were mostly middle-aged or older people. The younger generation would be there that night for the Heavy Weather concert.

Mitch didn't see Sally for the supper hour. He went back to his apartment to bathe, shave again and change into casual clothing. He was disgruntled that he hadn't thought to invite her to use his apartment to change in or nap or stay over.

What would she have done if he'd invited her to do that? She'd have looked at him as one of Dr. Frankenstein's rejects.

He had a light supper and finally went over to the center for the evening. He went around, inspecting the various Jamisons exhibits. They were all orderly.

The panties were still around the ankle of the model in Sally's booth. The fan still blew, the model still clutched her flying hat and her blank face gave no indication that she'd lost her drawers.

Pike came along looking rather the worse for wear. He was a little rumpled and he needed a shave.

On impulse, Mitch offered, "Do you want to go over to my apartment and freshen up?"

"Thanks, that's nice of you, but I'm going back to my own place. This has been a real drag."

"The Heavy Weather group will change your mind. Why not go over and rest a while? There's food for sandwiches in the refrigerator. Clean towels in the linen closet in the bath."

"Well, I just might."

Mitch looked at his watch. "I'll call you at seven, if you should go to sleep."

"Great. Thanks."

Mitch watched Pike walk away and knew that the impulsive hospitality might have been a mistake. Pike wasn't a top-notch employee and the time could come that Pike would have to be let go. Well, maybe he could encourage a better performance from Pike.

Mitch didn't think that would be possible. Pike hadn't much ambition.

So. Was ambition the only yardstick to measure a man? Or a woman? In the overall view of marketing and sales, it was.

For the exhibitors, there was again a buffet. Mitch couldn't find Sally anywhere. The Jamisons came to Mitch and said, "We just want to thank you for the way you handled that awkward situation."

Deliberately dense, Mitch asked, "Which one?"

"Miss Yoder's booth."

"Oh. I thought you were talking about all the carefully placed name cards being ignored at dinner last night."

"Yes. That was disappointing. You planned it so well. It was too bad that people couldn't have been a little more careful."

Mitch replied, "But everyone seemed to be having a nice time."

"Yes. That is true."

Another said, "The Yoder incident was on almost all the newscasts last night. And it was in the paper this morning. Did you see it?"

"Yes."

"Don't you think we should do something about that?"

Mitch said yet again, "How about discussing it on Monday morning?" Mitch considered that as shocked as the Jamisons appeared, none had removed the garment in question. That showed a bracing lack of interference. He added, "I honestly don't believe there's any problem."

"Yes. Well. We'll talk about it."

They parted, and Mitch went to a phone to call his apartment. The phone rang quite a long time before Pike answered sleepily. "Mitch?"

"Yeah, Pike, it's seven."

"Already?"

"Get a shower and come on over. There's still some food here."

"I'll be right there."

"Take a shower and shave. You'll be a new man."

"The old one suits me."

Mitch groaned and Pike laughed.

It wasn't until ten that the Heavy Weather band began to play. A sassy, fun women's group called Torch played lead-in. They flirted outrageously. The guys dancing loved it. The women were less enthusiastic.

But their last song was sung to the ladies. "Watch 'em, Honey," said it all.

Then the Heavy Weather band began. They started out onto the stage while the Torchers were still removing their instruments and the lead singer, Bill, sang to the departing women. Its title was "Get Out of My Life," one of Bill's own.

The song brought whoops from the men and punctuating calls from the women present.

Everyone was having fun. They all danced and moved and smiled and flirted. Sally didn't flirt. But her body moved and wiggled and, subtle as she was, men watched her. They danced with her. One was the cop.

Mitch didn't dance with anyone else. He stood and watched the dancers. Actually, he watched only Sally.

When Bill began his song, "Find My Love Again," Mitch went to Sally and stood threateningly by her partner. He told Sally, but he looked at her partner as he said, "This is my dance."

Mitch's attitude was so deadly that the guy just gave up. Sally wasn't paying much attention. Bill's song was so wonderful and so poignant that she was listening. They danced slowly, she and Mitch. He didn't say a word, but he held her. He moved her to the music and her body responded.

Bill's music touched something in Mitch and made him feel a yearning that had never been inside him.

He held Sally in his arms and felt empty.

Three

Mitch went back to his silent apartment and felt that he lived in a vacuum. He rewound the tape and played the newscast, fast-forwarding past the volcano eruption, the riot and the oil spill until they got to the crux of the half hour. He saw Sally.

He slowed her film and watched her. She was cool. She wasn't self-conscious or show-offy, she was professional. She was a cool point maker. She had done what she was supposed to do, she'd presented Jamisons products to an advantage.

It was a good saleswoman's pitch.

But that wicked wisp was also shown. Who would snitch them? The panties were over there at the closed and deserted Grand Wayne Center and anyone could take them and walk out with the wisp in his pocket.

Mitch got up, turned off the TV and the VCR and he went back to the center. He gave his Jamisons identification card to the guard, saying, "Just a personal check." He walked into the unpeopled room that was crowded with booths.

Mitch had no trouble and he did not even hesitate because he knew exactly where he was going. He went to her exhibit and the panties were actually still there.

He took the flimsy garment from the model's foot, put it into his pocket and left, bidding the guard a good-night.

There was no way that Mitch could allow some strange man to steal that bit of cobweb. It wasn't that he felt obligated to protect and defend that Busy Bee, he was simply taking care that an employee was not subjected to any further embarrassment.

Back at his apartment, Mitch had no idea what to do with the garment. He could hardly return them to the store, or to Sally, so he put the panties in his drawer. He closed the drawer and wished for a time lock.

He was tired. It had been an interesting but stressful weekend. Why had it been stressful? Well, the panty incident, of course, and the table mix-up, and the fact that Sally had plans for the Fourth.

So. She had plans. What difference did that make?

He undressed and brushed his teeth while he puzzled that out. He decided that his concern lay in the fact that the panty exposure might have given some guys the wrong impression of her. They might think Sally Yoder was a loose and receptive woman.

She was not.

Or was she?

Mitch went to sleep trying to decide which way he wished her to be. And his dreams apparently decided on their own. She was not at all demure. She shocked his sensibilities while his body loved it.

He wakened in a tumbled bed in a cranky humor. Surely he was more mature than that?

He went over to Rod's on Sunday afternoon and was smart enough to wear old jeans and a cotton pullover. The kids were up from their nap and ready to drive their parents wild.

As another of the Ohio Browns' take-in children, Mitch knew how to distract and entertain and teach children basics.

He took the kids outside with a dribbling hose and they watered...everything. It was done with little plastic watering cans that could be filled and carried by little kids—and the laughter. There is nothing like the laughter of little kids.

No one cared if they got wet or muddy or what they watered. The driveway, the porch, the side of the house, Mitch and even some plants got a share.

Mitch was elaborately shocked by being watered. Protesting, he picked kids up and ran with them. They laughed and laughed and laughed.

The white blond Rod lay back on a lounger and watched with a lazy smile. He encouraged, "Get them really tired so they'll sleep tonight."

"I'm working at it!"

And dark-haired Pat dozed and didn't mind having her bare feet watered.

Of course, the kids were wettest of all, and they were soon naked. One boy was almost two and the other boy was almost three. They looked like magical putti painted by the Italian artists of olden times.

Mitch found he would like to see how Sally handled such kids. How would she look at them and what would she do in response to them? And thinking that, he watched the two little ones with serious eyes.

Rod said, "You're thinking of a woman."

Mitch blinked, coming out of his trance, and looked at his older brother. "Now what made you say that?"

"You've been so different today, and I've been trying to figure you out. You've met a woman."

"I meet lots of women. They make up more than half of our population, they aren't shy, they run around everywhere and get into everything. How can I not meet women?"

Lax, his brown eyes interested, Rod replied, "You've met one that is different."

Mitch turned his head and looked up at the trees as if he were trying to recall meeting someone. And to be more honest with himself, he did try to think of some women besides Sally. "Probably at the Grand Wayne Center?"

"There?"

"I missed seeing you guys down there."

"We couldn't get a sitter. Twila and Pedro did a fine job with our display. We showed an axle, all shiny and new, with a wheel on either end."

"I checked it out. That was a good idea. All the ideas were well done. Simple, eye-catching—"

"None was as eye-catching as Jamisons."

"The houseware section?"

"Come on. Don't kid a kidder. You know I was talking about the panties. We saw it on TV, and I just wonder what the country is coming to with the *Jamisons* allowing something like that on TV to represent their store."

"You have to know they're shocked. We're slated for a meeting tomorrow morning about that very thing. But they may be a little more tolerant than their reputations. They didn't demand that the panties be removed. That surprised me. The little I know of them, it was a wonder that they didn't march right over there with their fire axes and chop the model apart and probably the perpetrator.'' Then Mitch said, ''You're too young to have been shocked.''

''My pregnant and prejudiced wife is sitting right over there.''

Pat didn't even open her eyes. ''I am pregnant, but I have no prejudice at all.''

Mitch exclaimed in a whisper, ''She listens with her eyes closed!''

''And even when she's asleep. She can hear through the walls from three rooms away with the door closed. The kids are going to be spooked when they realize they can't get away with *any*thing at all.''

''Are all women like that?''

Rod's lazy voice countered, ''Which one are you worried about?''

Mitch turned clear eyes toward Rod and replied with just the right amount of puzzled interest, ''None.''

Rod was rude enough to laugh.

And Mitch considered that the exact humor of the kids' laughter lay in the bottom of Rod's older, deeper laughter. It was such a natural, amused sound.

They had a light supper and Mitch went back to his isolated apartment. Even the air was vacant. There were no sounds on it. His furniture was static. His life was empty.

He stripped and showered before he got into the big, new bed and spread his arms and legs out. He was alone.

He got up and took the tape from its hiding place where no one would ever stumble across it at all and he watched Sally eating and smiling in slow motion and in freeze-frames.

Then he went back to bed and he finally slept.

On Monday morning, Mitch dressed in his most conservative suit, white shirt and a subdued red tie. He went to Jamisons and to his small, windowless office. The secretary he shared with a colleague told him, "Edgar Jamison asks if you will be able to come to his office about ten?"

Mitch nodded to the courtesy, "I'll be there."

She left his office door, and Mitch leaned back in his chair to think. Would they fire Sally? They might. Mitch was glad he'd removed the panties. He would hate to have had them thrust under Sally's nose, in accusation, in Mr. Jamison's office.

He worked with concentration to clear his mail and ten o'clock arrived too quickly. He walked down the hall and up the stairs to Mr. Jamison's office. Mitch's stride was strong and his mouth was set.

Mr. Jamison's office had a bank of corner windows.

All of the Messrs. Jamison were present. So was the culprit. She sat placidly waiting.

Mitch was the last one there.

"Ah, Goalong, glad you could come along." Edgar laughed.

The other Jamisons thought that was funny, too. Sally looked tolerant.

Mitch checked his watch. It was exactly ten. He smiled kindly and said, "Sorry I'm last one in."

Mr. Jamison mentioned the weather and asked if anyone would like coffee? And he said how fine the turnout had been for the exhibition. He also said how many comments he'd received on the bands, the Torch and Heavy Weather. "Everyone had a good time."

And to his own surprise, Mitch put in his oar. He said, "Sally's exhibit was remarkable. It was attention getting. I don't know how many women were sympathic over the model's lost garment. Women must have a rough time with clothing. Sally was especially smart in using that particular touchstone."

There was a stunned silence.

Sally handled it. She smiled at Mitch and said, "Thank you."

And Mitch plowed the silence with his added words. "The comments are coming in. We have letters from around the country. The writers must have seen the news on World News Network and written immediately. The response is very favorable. Miss Yoder has had two offers for jobs. Here's a cross section of the letters." He laid down three.

He'd exaggerated. Those were the only letters they'd gotten. But the three had really surprised HIM!

He said, "After all this fuss, maybe Miss Yoder should have a bonus of some kind."

She blinked one startled time and couldn't seem to look away from Mitch.

There was quite a thick silence, then Edgar said, "Well!" And he said, "Well, well, well!"

And the other Messrs. Jamison cleared their throats and neither of them appeared to be able to think of any comment one way or the other.

And Edgar finally smiled and said again, "Well, well."

Sally choked and had to cough discreetly to control her hilarity. Mitch's glance chided her, but he stood staunch and sober. His expression was of polite interest, as if the letters hadn't surprised him at all.

The Jamisons moved rather ponderously and exchanged judging glances as they tried to guess how to react.

And the senior Mr. Jamison picked up his cigar box and said heartily, "This calls for a cigar." He passed the box. And since there were seldom female Jamisons, he offered one to Sally.

She took it.

Mitch's eyelashes closed down over his sparkling eyes as he refused the box, and he wondered what on earth she'd do about the cigar.

She took off the wrapper before she rolled it between her fingers. Then she carefully snipped off the end. She had all their avid attention as she held it to the offered light and puffed the damned thing.

They were impressed until she began to cough. They grinned with male superiority which they shared, chuckling, as they exchanged glances.

The senior Mr. Jamison told Miss Yoder that she'd find a little something extra in her next pay envelope, and they closed the meeting.

Sally preceded Mitch from the room. She put the end of the cigar into her mouth between her teeth. She tilted up her chin and clasped her hands behind her back as she strode along the hall.

With a wicked, wicked glance and half smiling, she led Mitch to his office. They went inside and she closed the door after him.

Sally took the cigar from her mouth and ground it out in the clean, empty ashtray. Wiping her mouth on the back of her hand, she wiped that hand down her skirt. She went to Mitch and reached her hands up to the back of his head and kissed him right on the mouth.

She was against him. His body could feel the length of her softness from his mouth to his knees. It was as if his head was suddenly filled with bubbles. While he was entranced, he wondered if he would live through that stunning happening.

Releasing him slowly, she said, "You are a friend, indeed. Did you write those letters yourself?"

He replied soberly, "You taste like cigars."

"I'll gargle next time." Then she said, "Someone stole my French silk panties."

"What?" He was so stunned by her kiss that he could still seem stunned by her revelation.

"The ones in the exhibit."

"Oh." His gaze shifted and he took a careful step.

"Some *weirdo!*"

He was not! So he asked, "How could you be so sassy that you'd accept that cigar?"

"Mr. Jamison forgot that I was a woman for that one brief second. I had no choice but to take the cigar. To have refused it would have reminded him that I'm a dratted female, and that he has quotas looming in his conscience."

Mitch could understand that.

She smiled. "You backed me."

"You deserved it."

"Thank you."

"You're welcome."

She continued looking at him with that smile. Then she turned, opened the door and left.

Mitch sat down in his chair and found he was still recovering from her kiss. He felt his heart's pulse and found it quite high. He'd never paid any attention to his pulse beat before that minute. Health was something he could carelessly take for granted. Now he found his pulse rate was a little wild.

He became aware of the stench of the cigar, got up, took it to the men's room and started to tear it up before he flushed it away. But he stopped himself. It was a milestone in Sally Yoder's life. It was a symbol. He'd have it bronzed, put on a plaque, and give it to her.

Mitch took the cigar back to his office and found a partially eaten candy bar in a plastic box. He tossed the candy and entombed the stinky cigar in the box until he could have it bronzed.

Then he went to the rest room and washed his hands. As he washed them, someone glanced at him in question. Mitch remembered reading that, leaving a rest room, ninety percent of the women will wash their hands but only thirty percent of the men wash theirs.

Well, most of them smoke their cigars elsewhere.

The afternoon mail included two more letters concerning Sally. One did contain an inquiry on her availability. He gave the letters to Sally, but he gave the senior Mr. Jamison a copy of the one asking for her resumé.

He told the mail person, "I appreciate the fact that you have channeled the mail concerning Miss Yoder to me."

"I figured you'd do something about it. Any other way, and they'd have been shredded or some guy'd have blackmailed her before she coulda gotten her hands on them. Think she'll stay?"

Mitch dusted off a suitable-to-all-events Salty saying, "We'll see."

"Watching her makes coming to work worth-while."

"Better ration yourself. Don't be caught idle and get fired. I need you."

With that last sentence, the mail sorter slapped Mitch on his shoulder and knew they were friends.

So then, just before lunch, Sally came by his office and asked, "Lunch?"

He put a finger to his lips, got up from his chair, came around his desk and closed his door. "If we had lunch together this noon, they would be positive we're sleeping together—" He couldn't seem to get past those words. The very idea was stunning.

She nodded. "You're smart. I owe you a lunch."

He could only nod at the idea because something was wrong with his throat.

There were seven letters for Sally on Tuesday morning. Mitch split them again, giving the originals to Sally and giving Mr. Jamison copies.

That afternoon there were 115. One was a snarling, nasty one about women and their wiles and their primal disposition to flaunting themselves.

Mitch saw no purpose in showing the letter to either Sally or Mr. Jamison. He wrote a formal reply. "Thank you for sharing your opinion—" And he enclosed the letter back to the sender.

After work, Mitch took the cigar to have it bronzed. They thought Mitch was kidding. When he was firm about it, they were cautious with him.

On Thursday there were 437 letters. Nine were not nice. Forty-one were marriage proposals, and three proposals were obscene. He replied to those on his executive stationery beginning, "I am returning this to you—"

With the rest of the stack, he called a runner with a note to Sally, who was loose in the store, and invited her for a conference lunch in the directors' room. It would be vacant.

She accepted, "Thank you, kind sir. I would be charmed."

He read her stilted words and looked out of his door at the blank wall on the opposite side of the hall. Not even a picture was on that blah cream wall.

He realized, with sudden insight, that Sally Yoder was a trying woman. If he was to survive dealing with her, he would have to have something to look at when he was irritated or stressed or pleased with her— pleased?

And he leaned back in his chair, relaxing. Stretching out his legs, he crossed his ankles. He then lifted his hand and rubbed the top of his head while he mused on ways that she might please him.

At lunch, she discussed which of the jobs she might investigate.

Mitch was appalled! "You need more experience."

"I've been here six months."

"Six months is a drop in the bucket." He then said somewhat ponderously, as if dictating, "You will reply that you must honor your contract with us and that you will be in touch with them in six more months."

"I don't have any contract. You know good and well that—on Monday—the Jamisons would have fired me."

"There were the letters." And he amended, "There ARE the letters."

"Yeah. I made World News Network. I'm hot. 'Strike while the iron is hot' is good advice. I'm a two-

and-a-half-minute wonder. In six months, no one will remember the incident. Now is the time.''

She was right, of course. ''No.'' He couldn't look at her. ''You need more background. You need some further coup so that you're not a one-trick pony.''

''So. You believe that I've . . . shot my wad?'' Her mind veered and she inquired, ''Do you know that term of shooting one's wad comes from spitting tobacco juice and, instead of just the juice, they've spit out the tobacco? As I understand it, chewing tobacco takes a while to get the wad just right, so spitting it out by chance is a nuisance.''

He followed. ''I thought it was money at races.''

''No, when the saying started, there probably wasn't any paper money. Just tobacco.''

''They used tobacco for money?''

''It's possible.'' She shrugged. ''In trade?''

He inquired, ''Are we dealing in red herrings here?''

''Yes.''

''You don't believe you need any further experience?''

She eyed him with a very faint smile. ''In what?''

He lost track of his original line of argument. He could think only of how he could give her further experience. He said, ''Eat. We're running out of time.''

''For what?''

''Lunch.''

''Oh.''

So nothing was solved at all.

On Friday, Sally received 511 letters. Thirty-one were proposals of various kinds. There were a scattering of obscene ones and two were threatening enough that they were turned over to the FBI.

Naturally everyone at Jamisons was aware of how much mail was coming in from that Grand Wayne Center exhibition. In fact, just about everyone in Fort Wayne knew about Sally's mail.

All anyone had to do was pick up either paper on Wednesday. The post office mentioned the volume as it was delivered by bundle. The newspapers each took a picture of that. And damned if she didn't make World News Network again!

They did one of those follow-up blips. They showed Sally with her desk filled to overflowing with letters.

She looked so gorgeous and so vulnerable and so female that Mitch groaned over the additional male attention.

That weekend, Rod shook out the paper and asked Mitch, ''Is that the woman?''

Mitch didn't have to look at the paper's picture. He had five copies of it. He knew Rod meant was she the one from Jamisons. ''Yep. She's the one.''

''How's it coming along? Want some help?''

Mitch looked at his brother. ''Help?''

''We could have you two over for the weekend.''

''There's nothing between *us!* I thought you meant the replies to the letters Jamisons is getting. She's answering every single one personally.'' His response had been fine, up until then, but he added, ''She's keeping a file of the job offers.''

''Yeah?''

And he blew his facade of indifference. ''You should see the earnest marriage offers. Pictures, resumés, character references. You wouldn't believe it.''

''I think I would. I saw her on World News Network.''

Lamely, Mitch explained, ''She photographs well.''

And Rod laughed.

Such a sympathetic laugh rankled in Mitch. "We are not a couple. I mean nothing more to her than the mail clerk." And even as he said the words, he knew he had mischosen them. They sounded as if he wanted to mean something to her. He frowned.

Rod commiserated, "That is tough. I did everything, including dating other women, trying to avoid Pat. It was a waste of time."

"You have this all wrong. There is nothing between us."

"If we can help, let us know."

"Good God, Rod!"

"Peace, brother. Just know we're supportive."

"Back off!"

"I have. I have!" But he laughed again.

Mitch became withdrawn and aloof, but a man can't be that way long with two little boys tumbling around who don't realize a man is sulking.

Leaving the little boys with Rod, Mitch took Pat to a print store and she helped him to find some excellent prints copied from the masters. Pat explained about balance and about placing. She asked where the pictures would be and she had him observe the copies from that distance.

She made suggestions and found what Mitch wanted. The prints had been reproduced on canvas. One was of the series of van Gogh's *Sunflowers*. That would be on his office wall across from his desk. To one side, closer in order to allow Mitch to see all of it clearly, he would have a large copy of Brueghel's *Summer* showing the wheat harvest and the noon's rest time. And the large one for the hallway was a big windmill under a lowering sky by Rembrandt. They were to be framed simply, and Mitch would be notified when the pictures were ready to be picked up.

He desperately needed something to look at that would soothe his restless soul.

He'd taken the newspaper picture of Sally to the office and, staying late, he had used the copy machine at the office to acquire two excellent blown-up pictures of her. One was in his apartment's entrance hall so that she greeted him the minute he came in the door. And the other one was inside his closet door. At night he could open the door and see it.

He'd lost count of the number of serious men who had written and wanted to meet HER. But she now had about twenty-seven job inquiries. She also had an inquiry about a one-time lecture for a local business course in marketing.

She recommended Mitchell Goalong.

When he accepted, he hadn't known of her referral, and he'd been flattered with the invitation. When he discovered the truth, he was torn between being second choice and being thrilled that she considered him more experienced in marketing.

Then he was forced to consider that she had so much mail to answer that she just simply hadn't had the time to teach.

She had become the product of publicity. She was notable. She had a following. Men hung around her at work. The employees had done that, but now men came in as customers and wanted her attention.

Mitch rued the day he'd suggested the stores' public exhibition.

Four

Gradually, it came to Mitch that he had botched the perfect opportunity for firing the Busy Bee! The means had been given him on a silver platter with an apple in its mouth, and what had he done? He'd saved the nuisance's neck.

He sat at his desk and scowled at the excellent print of Brueghel's *Summer*. Somewhat disgruntled, he felt he ought to be in the picture, haying the field and eating a lunch brought out from the village by the women, just that way. Instead of sitting in his windowless office with the double B as a problem, he could be lying there in Brueghel's painted shade, digesting his meal, replete, watching the children playing and the women looking plump and ready to be plucked of their clothing.

Instead, here he was, harnessed with the charge of

controlling and getting rid of a woman who didn't really know her place in the scheme of things.

Was he a male chauvinist? More than likely. Why had he assumed he was a 1990's man?

His foster father, Salty, was all man—of course, he did do all of the organizing and cooking at the Brown household over in Temple, Ohio. While he did have an auto dealership there, it was all the other Browns who ran it, one way or another.

Mitch considered the fact that Salty was a retired navy man. He'd already done his macho share. And he was a better cook than Felicia, who floated around and was a Star in the Little Theatre there in Temple. She was helpless without Salty... or she made it appear that was so. She wasn't at all like Sally, that independent woman. Why not? Why did Sally have to be so different and difficult?

Temple had—what was it—somewhere around two thousand people? Something like that. And the helpless Felicia ran the theatre as her own. Yeah. It probably was hers. The Browns had more money than most people knew about. A clue to that was the fact that all the kids went to college. Mitch had his degree in marketing and the Browns had paid for it.

In the Brown household, Mitch had been a take-in child. He'd not been adopted. His divorced mother had been in a wreck and before her death she'd been in a persistent vegetative state as long as Mitch could remember. His surviving great-aunt was friendly, but she couldn't have taken care of Mitch. She, too, had been a helpless woman. There was a family friend who monitored her.

She'd had Mitch to visit in her big, gently deteriorating house. Those had been fascinating times for the imaginative Mitch. And when he'd gone out on his own, she'd offered him any furniture that he could use. Felicia had helped him choose a few pieces.

Felicia had said, "Maddie's things will all come to you eventually, but don't rush her. However, it's always nice to have a few really fine things around. Maddie won't miss this piece and it will be elegant in your apartment."

With Felicia's direction, Mitch had gradually learned to recognize the pieces he'd taken for granted at the Brown house.

Felicia and Salty had contributed several pieces to his apartment, a folding card table of rich cherry, and a marble-topped side table. There was a lamp from his Great-aunt Maddie that was pleasing to the eye and the colors hand-painted on the old glass globes were really beautiful.

The one rug he had from his aunt was Persian and very old. There had been no children's running feet to wear it down.

In his office chair, Mitch frowned at the Brueghel print and considered the women serving the men as it was supposed to be. And thinking how he wanted to be served, he realized that he hadn't seen Sally all day, that busy woman. He'd tried to run into her by accident, but she was always somewhere else, and he had no real excuse to track her down.

He should do that with an aphrodisiac-tipped dart gun, capture her, take her to his apartment and figure her out. Yes.

She was not in step with the rest of the world, and such a woman is dangerous in the business community. She could upset the applecart...and maybe even Mitchell Goalong.

The day was done. Mitch left the Jamisons building and walked over to his apartment. He wandered around his rooms and he felt alone.

That was the trouble with growing up in as big a bunch of offspring and adopted children as there had been, and were still, at the Brown house. A guy accepted the readily available company as normal.

Going out on his own and being by himself was like living on an alien planet.

He dialed Sally, the bee, and listened to her phone ring.

Did she have an answering machine? No. She wasn't that considerate. A man had to call and call and call and listen to her phone ringing in an empty house... apartment? Her address didn't specify which it was.

But then, she didn't know he'd been calling. If she had an answering machine filled with messages from him, that would be a dead giveaway that he was interested, right? Right.

He turned down several invitations. One from a friendly female customer who was cheerful and interested. One from the interviewer from the TV station. One from Pike, who was going fishing with a couple of guys. And Mitch had declined Rod and Pat's invitation for supper.

Mitch admitted that he wasn't living in a vacuum, he was isolating himself in case Sally should call. Where was she? Why should she call... him?

A sobering thought.

And the phone rang. It was Sally! It was a miracle. She said, just as if it weren't any kind of miracle, "Is your invitation for the Fourth still open?"

He was stunned. He managed to reply, "Yes."

"Oh, good. My plans fell through. I would love to go to the park and watch the fireworks from there."

"Good."

"I'll bring the food."

"Okay."

"That isn't inconvenient, is it?"

"No, no, no. It's fine. Really."

"Well, then, shall I drive in on Monday?"

"I'll come for you."

"It's the north half of the house."

"Yes."

"How did you know that?"

"I didn't. I was just acknowledging your information."

"Oh. What time?"

Right then! He hadn't said it aloud and he was stunned that he almost had.

She inquired, "Five?"

"Yes."

"Good. I'll see you then."

And he said, "Yeah."

She said, "Goodbye," and she hung up her phone.

He stood there with his eyes blank and the humming phone lax in his hand. He slowly put the phone into the cradle. She had turned him into a zombie. Was he no longer the master of his ship and the captain of his soul? Maybe not, he decided. And his imagination took over.

Would he really overthrow the government so that she could take over and be Sally One?

He probably would.

He should wait until Monday to ask her about that. Then he could find out if she wanted the whole country or just the middle part.

Most citizens of the United States thought the country consisted only of both coasts which were separated by a vast middle wasteland. After Mitch won that portion over for Sally, it would be years before either coast realized the middle of the country had become an independent queendom.

He wondered if she would allow him to be her consort. Maybe a captain of the guard? And if someone tried to overthrow her, he would spirit her away to his Aunt Maddie's moldering old pile of boards and they would live there happily ever after.

Happily Ever After was what Rod said Pat had given him.

Mitch wanted the same thing, but with Sally.

How could a man settle so quickly on an indifferent woman? Sally had given no indication that she wanted Mitch to overthrow the government or establish a queendom for her or any of that stuff. Why was he thinking that way? He didn't know.

Having forgotten that he'd refused Rod's invitation to supper, Mitch showed up there. Mitch noted that Rod laughed rather loudly when Mitch appeared at their door and that Rod turned and exchanged a telling glance with Pat, who smiled and very slightly shook her head, chiding Rod for some reason.

The two had communicated something between themselves in the manner of happily married people. Salty and Felicia had done that, too. And Mitch wondered if Sally was capable of that sort of exchange.

Ignoring his hosts, absently picking up Zeke, the two-year-old, Mitch considered if Sally could be on the same wavelength with a man. He doubted it. She was so engrossed in what she was doing at any time that she was totally unaware of any real contact.

Look how she'd been when she had set up that booth at the Grand Wayne Center. Her attention had been riveted on the display and she had only automatically responded to the greetings of others.

Mitch put Zeke down and picked up a clamoring Tod.

His remembering went on uninterrupted. Sally had walked past the displays to check out her own and when someone said something to her she'd nodded or lifted a hand, but she'd never really paid any attention to anything but the display. All response had been automatic.

Mitch sat down and put Tod off to one side as Zeke climbed up on his lap and began to go through all his pockets. Tod noted that and helped.

Mitch moved so that his pockets were available as he considered such absentmindedness proved that Sally couldn't ever be a good wife or mother. She just didn't have that necessary talent of attention to what was happening beyond what interested her.

The kids complained because Mitch's pockets were empty, chiding Mitch in sounds.

Without replying or soothing, Mitch reached into his back pocket and pulled out two squashed chocolate kisses.

Rod rumbled and took them from Mitch's hand just before the kids grabbed them.

Mitch didn't notice.

Rod said more firmly, "Mitch!"

"Hmmm?"

"You don't feed kids this age chocolate!"

Mildly, Mitch agreed, "Okay."

Pat called them to supper.

Rod and the little boys moved from the room toward the kitchen. Mitch walked toward the TV.

Rod called from the kitchen, "Mitch!"

"Yeah?"

"Supper!"

"Okay! Okay!"

He got up and went into the dining room to look around.

Rod said from the kitchen, "In here."

"Right."

He sat down and put his napkin on his lap. Then he put his elbow on the table and his chin on that and he looked out past the window at the recently child-depleted garden beyond the screened porch.

Rod gave Mitch a plate. Mitch set it down in front of himself and began to eat. He finished the meal at a normal eating rate, unaware of the exchange of comments between his brother and sister-in-law or their shared smiles. Having completed the meal, Mitch excused himself.

He stood up, and Rod followed him to the front door. Rod said, "I hope you bring her out to meet us. Pat says she believes she knows Sally."

"Sally." Mitch said the word in a caress as he walked out of their house to his car and drove away.

He never believed, for one minute, that he hadn't conducted himself normally.

He went back to his apartment, was greeted by her picture in the entrance hall, and went to the TV where he played her news tapes on his VCR. He smiled at her image and replayed the tapes.

He now had three brief tapings of Sally on television. They were all bits of newscasts. The last two were about the mail volume garnered by her first appearance on World News Network.

He went to the entrance hall and found himself standing in front of the enlarged-to-life-size picture of her face. He wasn't immediately sure why he was standing there, since that picture was black-and-white and the one on TV was in living color.

Finally he blinked a couple of times and frowned in concentration. He was there because his guardian angel was trying to tell him that if she came to his apartment on Monday she would see that picture.

He took it off the wall and carried it around for a while before he realized he'd have to hide it somewhere. He slid it under the bed in the spare bedroom.

On Saturday, Mitch looked more closely at his apartment. It wasn't too bad, but there was no rug in his bedroom. There wasn't one in either bedroom, only that lovely Persian one in the living room.

He needed a rug in his bedroom.

Someone had told Mitch about a great local rug dealer. The name was...uh...he went to the phone book and looked under rugs in the yellow pages.

There it was. Aaron's Oriental Rug Gallery. Right. Bob Anderson. Yes.

So Mitch left his apartment and walked over the six or seven blocks to Aaron's, and Bob Anderson was there. He said, "Hello."

And Mitch said, "I need a rug for the living room. I'd like a nice one."

So they looked through the collection with Bob explaining the varieties and types of knots and uses. How prayer rugs had a notch that should face the east. And it was obvious in no time that Bob knew his business.

Mitch didn't have the room for a carpet, but the ones Bob had were gorgeous. Mitch's decision came down to two rugs.

Mitch saw the rugs separately, described the furniture he had and considered that factor. He finally chose a beauty.

Wanting it at his apartment on Monday, he paid for it and carried it away, rolled, over his shoulder.

Bob Anderson smiled and allowed that, but his eyes danced with humor.

Mitch put his aunt's rug into his bedroom and the room was dressed. Then in the living room he unrolled the treasure from Aaron's and it was perfect on the oak floor.

Mitch had to walk around and view the addition from all angles. He was very pleased and smiled at the room.

His sofa was a cinnamon shade and there was the hint of that among the light browns and blacks in the patterns of the rug. An overstuffed chair was a dead brown that was a great accent.

He would get some long-stemmed yellow lilies for the light green gold-rimmed floor vase. He narrowed his eyes.

And he looked at the pictures on his walls and at the simple drapes and he was pleased. Would she notice the rug? The other had been on the floor when she was there. Would she notice the difference?

He called Rod and Pat to come to supper Sunday. They accepted.

Forgetting that Sally had said she would provide their supper, Mitch shopped and selected things he would have for Monday when she came to his place.

He was concentrating on those preparations when Rod called at four on Sunday, saying, "We'll be there in an hour for supper."

Mitch replied, "Great! I'm glad you called."

He greeted them like a good host and said, "What a surprise to have you drop by! And I'm glad you can stay for supper."

For some reason Rod laughed and shared the laugh with Pat. They didn't mention what was so funny. Mitch thought how cheerful they were and he wondered if Sally was able to share that kind of humor.

By then his guests had commented with delight over the new rug. They admired it and considered, and had to see how his aunt's rug was in his bedroom. They thought Mitch had chosen well.

The kids found the picture under the spare bed in the second bedroom and dragged it out into the living room. With great casualness, Mitch carefully put the picture into the front hall closet.

From the closet, Mitch then got a basket of toys he'd gathered for just such an occasion and the boys settled down, examining the hoard, trying to figure the toys out.

Pat said, "That was such a good picture of Sally—"

Mitch couldn't believe Pat would be so rude as to mention she'd noticed the revelation of a hidden picture that way. He handled it with élan, as if it were no big deal. His indifferent glance rested on Pat as if she hadn't made a gaffe.

Pat was continuing, "I saw Sally yesterday. She mentioned coming to town to watch the fireworks. Are you sure you wouldn't like to come out to us? There will be all the several neighborhoods gathered, and it'll be fun."

"No," Mitch replied. And even his subconscious knew that was not enough for Pat. He added, "Well, that's nice of you." Then he added, "Maybe next year."

And Rod choked.

Without ever knowing it was his "next year" so blandly said that had caused Rod's choking, Mitch gave Rod's back a couple of only reasonable whacks and Rod recovered. But Rod made the mistake of glancing a glint at his wife and he was set off again.

But then Pat laughed.

Mitch gave her an inquiring glance and Pat explained, "The kids are enjoying themselves so much."

Mitch frowned a little, looking at the quietly playing two, then he nodded a nothing response, and set about efficiently getting their suppers onto the table.

It was a pleasant evening. Mitch was aware of the subtle communications of togetherness that passed between Rod and Pat. It was very similar to that tie between Salty and Felicia, the adoptive harborers of their childhoods.

Rod's Zeke and Tod were busy and their activities were monitored and controlled by their parents. They weren't allowed to just run loose. Their parents did a constant supervision of the two without seeming to interfere at all. But they did.

"You're good parents." Mitch mentioned that in a thoughtful way.

"I had no choice," Rod replied. "I was trained from the minute I arrived on Salty's doorstep. You know he adopted Mike and John right after he got me."

"I seem to remember something similar. I was responsible for Cray and Tom almost immediately."

"You had Bob to help."

"God, he was a nuisance. He never wanted to let me be the leader."

"He's still that way. Salty's turned the six they have over to him, did you know that? They have Teller, who was a real challenge, and Bob solved him."

Rather pensively, Mitch asked, "Do you remember Tweed? I've always wondered what happened to him."

"Ask Salty. He always keeps in touch."

"Tweed was a real problem." Mitch thoughtfully chewed on his lower lip.

"Yeah. Salty grieved for a long time over him…that Tweed couldn't live there. That he needed to be free and solve his own life."

Mitch commented, "Salty may have grieved, but he never gave up. He'd find a way. Tweed probably still doesn't know Salty's been like an invisible guardian angel."

Rob laughed, "With that raspy voice!"

Mitch grinned. "When I got there, I wondered if I could handle it all. All those kids, and Felicia like a magical woman who wouldn't be able to handle anything."

"She's an iron lady in chiffon."

Pat commented, "Chiffon? How do you know that word?"

"You know Felicia."

Pat considered. "Yes. You're right."

Mitch asked, "Have you heard from Tweed?"

"Not for over two years."

"Doesn't that make you worry?"

"Not with Tweed. He'll show up some day, as if he'd been here just the week before. I never quit glancing down the street at night, half expecting him to be coming along in that stride of his. So...I Rule the World and I'm Pleased with It."

"That's it exactly."

Pat put in, "I've heard you mention Tweed. What a curious name."

"He chose it. Salty had a tweed coat that he especially coveted. And he liked the sound of the word. When he left, he took that coat along. Just about two years ago, Salty received a box and in it—"

Mitch exclaimed, "—was a tweed coat! Brief note, no address. I remember that! Salty's still wearing it."

"I know." Rod looked down at his empty plate.

Mitch's voice was gentle. "Salty loves you best. You were his first."

"I wish Tweed would come back. Salty is almost seventy."

"Tweed will surprise us, watch and see."

"Where do you suppose he is?"

"God only knows. Think what it meant to him to take that coat and to return one to replace it. A 'coat' of honor."

"Yes."

Rod was aware that Mitch had been more in touch with the conversation than he'd been with any for some time. Even that amused Rod. "We were lucky to have you stay with us. You taught us all to argue."

"It was Bob."

Rod grinned at Pat. "See?"

"I can't allow an untruth to spill out and take root."

"How noble."

"Pat. You do understand you're married to that man? You have to put up with him for the rest of his life."

"There are side talents that compensate."

"Sex." Mitch sighed.

"Well, now that you mentioned it, yes, but how did you know?"

Mitch indicated her slightly rounded stomach. "You didn't get that way by yourself."

"Do you mean this baby was caused by... sex?"

Mitch laughed and Rod said, "I'll explain it to you later."

Pat heaved a big sigh. "That again."

Rod said soberly to Mitch, "She only says things like that so people won't know what a sex fiend she really is." He looked pensive. "A man's lot isn't easy."

"Really?" Pat was fascinated. "Do you mean there are men who... are reluctant?"

"You hadn't noticed?"

They were still arguing as they helped clear the table, gathered up their children and left. They did remember to thank their host who felt a little as if he'd been a headwaiter and hadn't even gotten a tip. Or had he?

So the next afternoon he went to Sally's to fetch her back to his place. She came to her door carrying a wicker basket of her own and Mitch kissed her hello. She smiled and blushed a little and her eyes sparkled.

They went back to his car and drove to his apartment where he parked down on the street. He took the basket from her and carried it up to his place where he set it aside. He took her into his arms and kissed her really, really well. She not only allowed that, she helped.

He said, "My God, I can't believe you're here."

His voice smoked, his body burned against hers, and his eyes showed green flames. She saw that. She was amazed and looked at him with surprised interest.

He smiled harmlessly and inquired, "Does any of this need to be refrigerated?"

"Yes. But I've packed it with frozen pouches. It'll all last for hours."

"You're brilliant."

She smiled and moved rather elaborately as if modest.

And he chuckled in a manner that made her regard him again in a weighing way.

"Would you like to eat here? It's cooler. Then we could go down to the park to watch the fireworks."

"You do know that the fireworks are farther north? At Utilities Park near the coliseum? That's some distance from here. Do you really think we'll be able to see it from the pond in Freimann Park? Through the trees? The pond area with its benches is a little below the surrounding area."

He said innocently, "We can see."

She wondered how he meant that. They would be able to see or they would test the idea?

He smiled at her and said, "You're very good-looking." His face was benign and kind of swarmy with idiocy.

A little starchy, she retorted, "Nonsense."

"You fascinate any man."

"No. I'm just not interested, so I'm a challenge. Men are so predictable. Each feels he's God's gift to all women."

"Yeah. That about says it all."

"So you admit that you think you're every woman's dream?" She watched him soberly, waiting for his response.

"We weren't talking about me. We were just discussing you and men."

He'd slid out of that one. She gave him enough rope to hang himself. She asked, "Do you feel that you are different from other men?"

"I'm an observer in the March of Time."

She had to laugh. But she was aware that this male was different. He was dangerous for a disinterested woman because she could let down her guard and consider him as a human.

Five

———

Exquisitely, and very basically human, Mitch shivered inside his skin, acknowledging he was only a man. His cells all danced with the awareness and his testosterone level was urgent with the message that not only was he a man, she was a woman.

As any cautious man who is partially civilized would do, he smiled at Sally as if he were harmless.

She wasn't stupid. She recognized the danger. And still, she stayed. But she was in control. She didn't take his hand and coax his carefully reluctant steps into the bedroom.

She said, "If we had a big mirror, about fifty feet wide...no, about a hundred feet wide, we could put it up so that its view cleared the roof and the buildings, and we could see the fireworks."

He guessed, "You really don't think we can see from the park."

She smiled.

He took a deep, patient breath, licked away his smile from his mouth and took a step across her path. "I believe there's a saying about 'Ye of little faith.'" He cast a casual sparkling, teasing glance her way that was filled with temptation.

She lifted her chin and her own eyes were naughty with teasing. "We—"

And someone rang his doorbell from downstairs.

Mitch frowned at the interruption. And waited.

Sally gestured toward the door and lifted her eyebrows.

He put his finger to his lips in a silencing gesture.

The ring came again. Then a voice called through the speaker, "Mitch? I brought you some fish!"

Mitch knew Pike wouldn't leave easily. He whispered, "Go in the bedroom." He took her arm and started her on the way. "Close the door."

"That's Pike."

"Sh-h-h."

Sally went into Mitch's bedroom, closing the door, and she looked around. She saw the fine rug had been moved into his bedroom. She considered the pictures on his wall and thought how much he had made the apartment his. Then she opened his closet door...and she saw her picture.

She stared at it a minute, experiencing emotions from surprise to annoyance to—something different that went through her. She gently closed the closet door, went to the window and looked out, unseeing, listening to Mitch being minimally cordial with Pike. She heard their voices go into the kitchen, then return to the living room.

"Sorry to rush you," Mitch was saying.

"You got somebody here?" Pike's voice penetrated into the bedroom.

"No. I'm on my way out."

"Oh, I'll walk along to your car."

"I'm not quite ready to go. I still have a few things to do."

"Can I use your can?"

"Uh, sorry, I was just cleaning and there's a mess."

"Oh." Pike paused. "Yeah." His brain was working. "Uh."

"Thanks for the fish."

"Sure thing."

"See you tomorrow."

"Yeah. Sure. Mitch, do you want to come along to see the fireworks at our complex? It's really pretty and there's always room for one more, if you haven't anything else to do."

"I'm going to my brother's."

"Oh. Good. I didn't want you to spend the day alone."

"Thanks, Pike."

"See you tomorrow."

"Yes."

"Hope you like the fish."

"I will."

"Well, I'll be going."

"Yes."

And Pike finally left.

Mitch closed the door as Pike's steps went down the stairs. Mitch listened to the lock click, with satisfaction, and he turned toward his bedroom door where Sally was hidden . . . And he remembered his picture inside his closet door. My God! he thought.

He went carefully to the bedroom door and hesitated in opening it. He tapped. "Sally?"

"Yes."

She didn't come to the door. Mitch's libido quivered. She was naked, spread out on his bed and waiting for him. He took a very unsteady breath, as his brain scolded him for the fool he was.

With decision, he opened his bedroom door, saw the empty, neat bed and glanced immediately at the closet. The door was closed. He looked at her.

She was standing with her back to him at the window, looking off down the street as the traffic went on west.

"It was Pike."

"I heard."

"He wanted to use the bathroom."

"You have two."

"I didn't want him to know you were here."

She turned. "I heard."

"Pike can't keep anything to himself."

"No."

"In the scheme of things, it's better if no one knows we see each other outside of Jamisons. It could be awkward."

"I see."

They faced each other, he at the door of his bedroom and she across the room by the window at the head of his bed. He asked carefully, "What do you 'see?'"

"Knowing me—socially—makes you uncomfortable."

"How can I protect you as an interested man? You are more secure as a co-worker." With his regard on her continuously, he went slowly across the room, around the foot of the bed, to stand in front of her. "Sally."

She gave him a cool glance. "Mitchell. Or should I say, 'Mr. Goalong?'"

He took a deep breath and pushed his hands into his trouser pockets. He gave her a disgrunted look and commented softly, "I may throttle you."

"How typically male."

"How can I be otherwise? I am male."

"I had noticed."

He watched her. "And?"

She smiled just the tiniest little bit, but she didn't reply.

So he pulled his hands from his pockets, pulled her to him and he kissed her.

He wrapped his arms around her, held her tightly and he was agonized by the fact that she was against him after that almost separation. What would it be like to lose her? And he realized that he was getting very possessive thoughts about this woman whose arms were around his shoulders and whose soft body was relaxed against his tensed one. He wanted her in a way that was different.

He wanted to love her body in the obvious manner, the difference was the wanting wasn't just raw need or curiosity or something obvious. The need he felt was different.

Why was her body so precious? Why was her mouth so special? Why did he consider her more beautiful than any other woman? And he remembered thinking that she was average. How foolish he had been.

So he did the only thing he could think to do: he kissed her with the seriousness of his longing. His arms held her with tender violence of true need. He trembled and his mouth was greedy and his hands were stiffened and carefully, gently harsh.

His muscles became rigid with iron and his bones melded with steel. His lungs turned into leather because flesh of no sort would handle the fire he breathed. All that was so because he felt it happen.

She made little noises and his steel and iron became as gentle as such can be. He asked, "Have I hurt you?"

She gasped, "Not yet."

Panting furnace blasts, he swallowed liquid fire and shivered. Even his hair trembled, and his sex was tight and urgent. He recognized that he must release her before he did something they would both regret. He tried. He put his head back and gasped with his effort, but he couldn't let go of her.

She gave a little squirm, indicating that she wanted to be released.

He was baffled because he didn't know the signals to relay to his arms and to his eagerly concentrated body.

She again moved to be free. And he was annoyed that she could kiss him in that all-stops-out way and still be in control of herself. He frowned a little and stared hotly at her, still filled with steam, hot ash, iron and steel, and breathing with leather.

She said, "Why do you have my picture in your closet? To frighten mice or to discourage other women?"

He said the first thing that came to mind. "Mice." He was a little distracted by the icy sensation that was sizzling on his white-hot steel and iron skin causing it to steam and cool.

"You think I'm a cat?"

He was on rote. "A bee."

She had gained enough space so that she could lean back a little and look up into his face. "Do you kiss all bees that way? It's a miracle you aren't all bitten up."

His mind elsewhere from the conversation, he replied, "I am. It just doesn't show."

"Any man who kisses the way you do has had a great deal of experience. I feel beyond my depth."

"You're the first woman I've ever wanted."

"Pah!"

He was cooling more. "How can you be so in control when I'm a shambles. Do you go around attacking men that way just so you can see how bad the wreck will be?"

"Of course not. I've never been curious bef—"

He waited. When she didn't continue, his arms tightened just a fraction. "You were experimenting? That's playing with fire. Not matches, but the real thing."

"No. I only wanted a kiss."

"I have others. Different kinds."

"I believe you are a roué. I think you've left a trail of devastated women behind you. You probably had to leave some town before you came here."

"No. I'm a good man."

"You kiss like a wicked one."

"I've never kissed that way before in all my life. It was you." He was very serious. "Kiss me again."

"I wouldn't dare."

"I dare you."

"I don't follow dares. It only gets a woman in trouble."

"I'm the recipient. I have to be the one to cope. I was beyond restraint, but you were cool as could be. You were the one who stopped us."

She reached up and smoothed his hair back. "Thank you for stopping. I was boggled."

"Were you?"

"I shouldn't tell you that."

"Oh, yes. Don't have it be only me who was tempted."

"I didn't mean to tempt you."

"Did you bring up that picture I have of you, just to shock me?"

"Yes."

"What were you doing in my closet?"

"I wanted to see if you were tidy."

He laughed and hugged her sweet body to him with a groan.

"Let go."

"In just a minute."

"You must."

"I know. It was close."

She nodded.

His voice was ragged. "But not nearly close enough."

"Too close. We must be careful."

"Why?"

"Because we're susceptible."

His arms tightened, his eyes closed, and his body was excessively sensitive as he groaned. "Yes."

"You need to let me go."

It took a while for Mitch to convince himself. He took breaths and moved his head as if he were going to argue, but he did begin to release her. Slowly. "God, I hurt."

"Think about something else."

He groaned. "How like a woman to say something like that."

She remembered telling him that he was a typical male. He was. He was. To give him something else to distract him, she asked, "Are you hungry?"

He laughed with some helpless irony. "Not for food."

"I'm trying to help you."

"That's a good attitude." His eyes and voice were smoky. "I'll show you how." And he took her back against him and kissed her until her brain dissolved.

He had her gasping and her fingers clawing at his shoulders when he set her on her feet and held her steady. "Sorry, honey, but I couldn't be the only one hurting."

"I knew it! You did that deliberately!"

And he smiled. His eyes were hot and his hands were scalding on her arms, but he held her steady and he didn't repeat his temptation.

Sally leaned her head into her hands and groaned. "That wasn't kind."

"I know."

"You could have resisted."

"But if I had, you wouldn't know what I'm dealing with."

"You beast." Her tone was conversational and her eyes were closed, her mouth was vulnerable.

He watched her.

"I think we should go to your brother's, just as you told Pike."

"Really?"

"Please."

"I had no idea you were such a coward."

"It's not cowardice, it's that susceptibility I mentioned."

"If I've really whammied you, how can you make verbal sense?"

"I have no idea."

"Do you have any clothes that are a little more childproof than those?"

"At home."

"We can't go there. The traffic across town will be horrendous. We'll have to see if you can wear something of mine."

He opened the closet door and there was her picture. "I look at you before I go to sleep."

She was solemn.

"You don't object when I do that. You melt in my arms and love me."

"Probably."

He paused and looked at her. "Probably?"

"If I had a picture of you inside my closet, you'd do that."

"I'd materialize and climb into bed with you."

"Surely not."

"Emphatically."

"You'd have more restraint."

"No. Here, try this."

It was a pair of sweatpants with a drawstring. She held it against her and agreed, "It'll fit."

He located some T-shirts and allowed her to choose one. Then he said, "I get to watch you change."

"No."

"You need to open your mind to new adventures. You need to be more receptive to new ideas. You need—"

"You need to go get the picnic basket and call your brother."

"The phone's in here." He smiled and indicated it. "There's another in the kitchen."

"You are observant."

"Shoo."

"I'll go in the kitchen and I'll watch you undress."

She looked around. "How?"

"In my mind."

"Distract yourself."

"Why would I do a stupid thing like that?"

"Because you must." She watched him very seriously. "We don't know each other well enough to be this far along."

He smiled and bit into his bottom lip.

"Go along, Goalong."

He groaned.

"You've heard that before?"

He admitted, "A couple of times, but the problem is leaving you here alone. Look at my waiting bed."

"It looks like any bed."

"It's paradise." His voice was grave. "Come see if it isn't."

"Who writes your dialogue?"

"You do, in my mind."

She guessed, "You believe I want you?"

He nodded, adding, "If you'd admit it to yourself."

"Why?"

"Because I tempt you and you don't want to resist me. You want me to control myself while you experience your reaction to me as you taste me to your limits."

"Actually, I think you're right. I beg your pardon."

"I have an iron will. You can taunt me as much as you like. I give my permission to you to have a free hand in exploring your susceptibility."

"Wow! What a lure. And your word choice is exquisite. And if I push too hard, then you just say, 'Shucks!' Right?"

"I hadn't thought of the actual words. Probably 'Oops' might be better, because I couldn't even pretend to regret the slipup." He smiled like a satyr.

"Go call your brother."

"Need any help with buttons or zippers?"

"No. Thanks, anyway."

"Stockings?"

"I can handle it."

"So can I. That is, I could learn the skill. Such knowledge would expand me as a man." And he laughed.

She said, "Get!"

"Kiss me goodbye."

"You're only going into the kitchen to call your brother."

"Being even a room away from you is too far."

She laughed a delightful sound of humor. "What a line!"

"It's true."

She scoffed. "Nonsense."

He soberly considered her for a minute and he knew what he'd said was indeed true. That was stunning, to recognize he was serious. Soberly he turned and went out of the bedroom, closing the door after him.

She was still standing by the window. Her face was still. She frowned a little and lifted her chin as if her thoughts went far into the unknown distance. She looked at the tempting bed and frowned, tightening her mouth at it. Then she went over and shifted the lock on the door before she began to undress.

Rod and Pat were delighted with the addition to their group. The four adults and two little ones walked over to the park. It wasn't far. Sally led the three-year-old Tod until Rod picked him up and effortlessly carried him and the picnic basket on one opened chair.

Sally glanced often to monitor Mitch who carried Zeke, a ground cloth and the other basket. Men's muscles were just so different. Their bodies—Sally carried two of the light folding chairs. Pat carried one.

That year, being Browns and with the letter *B* in the first third of the alphabet, they were to supply a vegetable for the feast.

After refrigerating the contents of her picnic basket, Sally had thrown together a casserole of undiluted mushroom soup, a jar of mushrooms, green beans, crushed potato chips and garlic salt. It looked like seaweed laced with spume and dotted with fragile shells. It was delicious.

The second third of the alphabet contributed salads and the last third brought desserts. The associations provided the meats, beverages, paper cups, plates and napkins.

People spoke to Rod and Pat as old acquaintances, making Mitch realize how long Rod had been in Fort Wayne and in that area. He glanced over at Sally and wondered if she—

And someone called to her. Then others called. And their eyes were lively on Rod and Mitch. Since each man was carrying a child, it was difficult to pair Sally with one.

Mitch got territorial. He moved over beside Sally. He was staking his claim? He was just sorting out who was with Sally.

The foursome chose a place. Mitch spread the ground cloth and they settled down. Pat and Rod were old neighbors and had been to the association parties—Well, Pat had. Rod had never attended until last year.

But people called to him and reached to touch his shoulder and chided and teased like old acquaintances. And they admired and spoke to the little boys.

Mitch had known of Rod's life with his late wife Cheryl. The pair had been very isolated by Cheryl's long decline. But the neighbors had always felt Rod was their neighbor. And their kindness to Rod after her death had been talked about in the Brown family.

Mitch put Zeke by Tod, between Rod and Pat, subtly designating them as a unit. He and Sally were separate. He felt he'd been subtle and clever. Rod and Pat slid glances to each other and tried not to smile.

Then Mitch was less subtle. After the meal, he helped clear away, then he took Sally's hand and pulled her to her feet to stroll around as they waited for the late darkness of summer so that the fireworks could be seen.

Mitch liked the women's voices that called to Sally, but he didn't smile when male voices demanded her attention.

And as those male voice surfaced as flesh-and-blood men and came to chat with Sally, Mitch didn't release her hand.

But then, she didn't wiggle her fingers asking to be released.

A couple of the men asked if she was in the phone book? And she replied that she was. But she didn't smile and suggest that they call.

Mitch stood silently and didn't smile or enter the conversations. He looked at the men as if they'd better not step too close.

After one such encounter, Sally said, "You're not far from being a very basic male. What cave brags on your birth?"

"It's in Ohio. I'll take you there so you can see it."

"I needn't see the actual one. I accept that it was so."

"You're not surprised?"

"No."

"Why?"

"I've never seen such a basic male as you present yourself."

"Because I wanted you in my bed?"

"Because you're making everyone here think we're a couple."

"Are you old enough to flaunt that? Aren't you afraid of scaring me off?"

She gave him a sliding side look and replied, "My fingers are permanently crippled from being crushed every time a male voice says my name."

"I did that?"

"Yes."

And he had the gall to reply, "Oh." He picked up her hand and carefully examined her fingers, frowning at them, flexing them. "There's no permanent damage."

With a great indrawn sigh, she looked at the sky to share that great put-upon patience, and he laughed.

They probably walked among or around every single person who had gathered there that evening. By the time they returned to Pat and Rod, no one could have missed the fact that Sally was with a particular man. And with questionings, the news was exchanged that he was Rod Brown's brother, Mitchell Goalong.

Sitting on the groundsheet with his brother and family, Mitch was imbued with a feeling of success. As the night became darker and the park lights were shut off, the fireworks began.

The two little Browns wakened and watched, owl-eyed, each held by a parent.

And Mitch lay back and brought Sally down beside him. He arranged her so that her head was on his shoulder, so his arm was around her. He thought it was dark enough. Actually, he hoped it was obvious. Anyone not watching the fireworks but watching the people could see them well enough in the bursts of colored lighting.

With the show's end, the carrying baskets were collapsed and tucked into chairs. Each man carried a drowsy child and chairs, and they went back to Rod's house.

Of course it was Pat's house. Ever since the pair had been married Rod's house had been vacant. Sitting across the driveway, it sat dark and empty.

The kids were rinsed and rolled into their beds. The adults said good-night and Mitch and Sally left.

Because Mitch was the calculating man he was, Sally had to go back up to his apartment to sort out her food to take it all back home.

Unarguably, he stated, "I can't eat all that food. I'm not here."

"Neither can I. I'll split it with you."

"We could eat here tomorrow and the next day."

She gave him a patient look. He hadn't suggested that until he had her inside his apartment. "I could bring lunch for the next couple of days."

"No." He shook his head. "Even if we went out into the mall and ate on a bench, fifty people would see us and mention it."

"We could have a conference lunch to discuss my unprecedented behavior?"

"Too late. Everyone's used to you."

"Are they really?"

"Since the mail has slowed down a little, you've dropped into second place on the gossip listing."

"We'll have to think of something to revive me."

"My desktop?"

"With the glass on it, everything would slid right off."

"In the film, *Bull Durham*, they fell off the very bed."

"How interesting you instantly remembered that!"

"Well, I can't think of any other reason for us to be on my desktop and sliding off."

"The food."

"You put it in a salacious way."

"I did nothing of the sort!"

"Why would food slide off a desktop?"

"I'm still 'seeing' them falling out of bed in *Bull Durham*."

He took a deep breath and rubbed his chest as he walked around.

"I'll hurry."

"Doing . . . what?"

"You're impatient. I'll leave. Oh, you have to drive me. Sorry."

"What IS the matter with you?"

"Aren't you impatient for me to leave?"

"I'm going crazy with wanting you."

She gestured widely and leaned over to say, "We don't even know each other!"

He soothed her. "We'll get acquainted along the way."

"Has this scenario ever worked?"

"Not yet."

Six

___

In Mitch's kitchen, Sally busily sorted out the foods they would leave at his place. She returned very little food to her own basket.

Mitch objected, "Honey." His tongue so savored naming her that he almost could taste the word. "I won't eat all of that."

She straightened and looked at him and tightened her mouth. "I had assumed that we would eat it. I don't eat this much."

"You can leave it here, but you have to swear on your honor that you'll come home with me every night this week and help me eat it up."

She allowed her eyelids to cover her guilty delight. She studied her fingers as if she needed to assimilate his demand and decide what to do about it. She was brave. She lifted her chin and tilted her head a little, several ways, before she summoned an agreement from her vocal cords...just barely. She said with great and noble acquiescence, "All right."

He relaxed a little and he almost smiled.

She charged him, "No hanky-panky."

His eyes widened with innocent shock. "Of course not."

"This is strictly so the food doesn't go to waste."

He nodded. "Right."

"You're not to lure me."

"Never." Then he added, "I get good-night kisses."

"I'll...think about it." She would. She would.

"A man can't ask more than that."

She gave him a quick look.

His face was sincere.

He carried her basket down to his car and put it on the floor of the backseat and her into the passenger seat. The street was dark and quiet. The traffic was thinned to nothing. The buildings were silent, the streets deserted. Sally thought it was a little scary.

She noted that, while Mitch looked around, he didn't appear to be unsettled. He walked around the car and got into the driver's seat.

She said, "The streets are deserted."

"Not much traffic, this time of night."

"It's dangerous."

"Naw."

"I do read the newspapers."

He dismissed trouble. "We have patrols."

"Do you ever walk at night?"

"I jog."

"That seems foolish."

He turned out an opened hand. "No more here than anywhere else."

"I'd rather you didn't."

"Didn't . . . what?"

"Go out on the streets at night."

"It's quiet, no traffic, nobody."

"There might be."

He was serious but gentle. "You can't live your life with 'might be.'"

"You can't be foolish either."

"Are you worried about me?" His voice had become husky.

She got snippy again and tilted her head some more. "For the rest of this week, I have committed myself to helping eat food that is stored in your kitchen and I've already decided to use my grocery money for that brown suit in the exhibit, so if you were harmed I would have to eat at home and I wouldn't get the suit."

"Oh."

She laughed.

"I've never felt so . . . unnecessary."

She agreed, explaining, "It's the food."

"I could just give you the key and you could go in alone and eat your share."

"How would I give you the good-night kiss you've specified?"

He gave her the wickedest glance she'd ever witnessed. "I could collect them all at once on the last night when you returned my key."

She accepted that premise with an airy, "I suppose."

In a low, almost growling voice he told her, "I've never before met a woman who needs a man's hand on her as much as you do."

She scoffed. "Ho!"

"Yeah."

They had reached her house. She'd left a light on. Her neighborhood was silent, the streets vacant. He slowed the car to a stop and looked around. He got out of his side of the car and moved around it, looking around. He opened her door, unlocking it, and gave her his hand.

She got out and stood silently.

He got the basket from the back floor of his car and turned to carry it inside. He said, "The streets are deserted."

"Okay, Mitchell, you make your point."

"You recognized the quote?"

She started up her walk to the door. "We, too, have patrols. Concerned Citizens' Watch. I'm a member."

Very quickly he demanded, "Who rides with you?"

"Various people."

"Who?"

"I'll give you a list."

They had reached the door. "I get a kiss."

She unlocked her door and went inside. He followed. She inquired, "Haven't I kissed you several times today?"

"Not yet."

She turned and began, "I recall—"

But he didn't need a recall, he needed to hold her against him and kiss her. He did that. It was stunning.

Their bodies glued together and their mouths fused and lightning cracked, parting the sky. Thunder rolled and cosmic chaos threatened. The lovers reeled apart in the odd silence and they were stunned. He rocked on his heels and she clung to the doorjamb. Their breaths were harsh.

"Who are you?" he asked hoarsely.

That she managed to reply literally, "Sally Yoder," was proof enough of her disastrous condition. Who was she? He knew who she was. Why had he asked that? "Why?"

"Who put you here, on this planet, to cause the sundering of the ecosystem you just accomplished?"

"It wasn't I, it was you!"

"You're a dangerous woman."

"I won't come to supper tomorrow."

"Don't weasel out of that. I have to keep a hand on you until I figure out what you're doing on this planet. Wasn't there a movie called *The Bee Girls from Outer Space*?"

"I have no idea."

"They turned the men into drones."

"Right."

"Is that what you're doing?"

"Sure."

"You get us all chasing you and the top flyer gets you? Who's my competition?"

But her reply was smothered by his second kiss. It was worse. Better. Stupendous.

She put her hand to her head and moaned, "Don't. I can't handle another."

"Another...what?" His voice was hoarse.

"Kiss."

So he kissed her again, but not on her mouth. He moved his head slowly as he kissed her cheeks and her nose and her forehead and her chin and under her ear. They were soft kisses and totally unfair.

Her breaths were broken.

He heartlessly released her and said, "See you in the morning."

She stood as he left her. He tested the door and looked at her. Then he walked through the doorway, pulled the door tightly shut after him and he left.

He got into his car and went back to his apartment, put on jogging clothes and went out to run for quite a long while. The patrols and the cops were used to him, by then, and Mitch waved in reply.

The next morning, dressed carefully and shaved meticulously, Mitch drove to Sally's to take her to work.

She was impatient. "What are you doing here?"

He smiled at her surprise. "I'm your...ride...for today."

She pushed at him so that she could close the door in his face. He didn't move easily. She said, "Don't be a cretin. You're the one who said no one at Jamisons should know we see each other outside of the building. We show up together and...that's IT!"

He went blank. "Oh."

"I'll see you tonight at your place. For supper." She gave him an impatient glare and closed the door.

There he was on her front steps, rejected. He took his carefully shaved face back to his car and, deep in thought, he drove to Jamisons. Women were weird.

He was busy, so he didn't see Sally all that day. He was surprised that the day passed fairly quickly, and he went home eagerly.

She was late.

He'd about given her up when his doorbell rang. He punched the release button and opened his door to go down the stairs to meet her.

She was hot and tired and a bit cross. He didn't say anything. He turned and walked beside her, back up the stairs, and escorted her inside his apartment. He went into the kitchen and handed her a well-aired glass of wine. He said, "Sit down. It's ready."

She didn't argue. She sat and sipped.

He served the perishables: potato salad and slaw. He'd bought a couple of delmonico steaks and, predictably, hers had to be cooked a little longer. The hot-dog buns had been cut diagonally, opened, spread with a little butter and a lot of parmesan cheese and toasted.

She ate thoughtfully. The silence stretched and finally she said, "You're hired."

He glanced up, raising his eyebrows with some questioning interest.

"You won't have to do windows."

He tightened his mouth in disgust and sighed as he shifted in his chair.

"This has been an awful day."

"Why?" He encouraged.

"Do you believe the Jamisons are inclined to rigidity?"

He appeared to consider that. "I think that might be possible."

Her eyes twinkled as she gave him a tolerant look.

"What'd they do to the Busy Bee today?"

"On the sale board at the entrance? I put a single sample of everything on sale in the women's department." She moved her hand in circles as she listed them, "A shoe, it was a red high-heeled one hooked over the top of the board. A suit jacket that's black with silk edging hung from one corner. The sleeve from the blouse peeked from under it. The bottom of an ecru lace slip showed below that. And there was a fedora. The Jamisons removed those. They chided that I was interfering with the other sections."

Mitch sat back and said, "It was brilliant!"

She gestured. "In a glance, people could see the bargains. Edgar said the newspaper advertising clippings posted on the board were good enough and discreet."

He shook his head slightly. "But people aren't as used to newspapers as they are to TV and the instant communication of a picture."

She agreed. " . . . and in living color."

"I think you've got a good idea. You have to realize that you're supposed to report to me? I'm supposed to screen these ideas. This one is very good and I'll follow up on it. You'll get credit."

She put up a thumb. "I'm for success."

That sobered Mitch. What would she consider as success in a man? With her busy mind and innovative brain, could she "see"—him? He was uncertain. She'd never mentioned her innovation to him, the head of marketing. "What a busy bee you are," he observed rather soberly. "Next time, run any ideas by me first."

"I keep forgetting we have you with us to do that sort of thing. I beg your pardon. I will tell you next time."

She would "tell" him "next time." Now what did that mean? She planned to continue going on, bullying her way through? Taking over? She was a maverick. A wild hare. He needed to channel her into the mainstream so she wouldn't upset the applecart. And he was bemused by all the clichés he'd just used.

She finished the last bit of toasted hot-dog bun and sighed in contentment. She sat back and smiled at him. "This has been one of the nicest dinners I've ever had."

"I liked the company."

"You were very kind to me. You didn't talk or nag or push."

"I have great control."

She laughed at him.

She was treating him like a houseman. Maybe having her to his place and providing the meal wasn't that good of an idea. He was setting himself up to be considered in a different way than he wanted her to see him.

He said, "Now I get my good-night kiss."

She regarded him with caution.

With that reaction, he thought, maybe she hadn't been misled. She was aware that he was a male. He rose from the table as she busily gathered plates and began to clear away. He stood, patiently watching her.

With the kitchen tidy, the dishes in the dishwasher and the foods put away, she then snatched up her purse and said, "Good night," as she headed for the door.

His legs were longer; his arms reached farther. He stopped her just through the door into the living room and pulled her against him. He kissed her. He heard the thud of her purse hitting the floor as her hands crept slowly up to his shoulders and then went around the back of his head.

Her body against his was wonderful and he showed no careful consideration of her female sensibilities. He pulled her tightly to him, down the length of him, their knees touching at various levels against one another's legs. Their bodies were pressed together, her breasts at the bottoms of his ribs in sweet softness. His hard sex was against her lower stomach, making her aware of him.

She gasped air as he lifted his mouth to look at her very seriously. Eyes were closed, reddened lips parted, moving helplessly, her head lay back on his arm.

He knew he should release her so he kissed her again. It was all just nerve-racking and intense and disturbingly marvelous. He shivered.

Her lips formed the words. "Let...me...go."

Such soft, hesitant words. He loosened his arms in some surprise that he could. He was still considering that when she lifted her mouth for another kiss! She did!

So, being a fool for danger, he kissed her again. It was worse. They got tangled up and panting and wild-eyed and disorganized. Chaos.

When he lifted his mouth from hers so that he could breathe desperately for oxygen or control or something, she moaned softly.

He trembled and turned into the iron/steel/leather man again. His breaths were harsh and he was surprised flames didn't rush out of his mouth as he exhaled.

She said, "I must go. Help me."

Help...her? How?

She indicated he was to let go of her. So he did that and then had to steady her. She turned vaguely, apparently searching for something.

He asked, "What do you want?" She would reply: you. His steel/iron arms would scoop her up and he'd carry her—

She said, "How do I get out?"

"Of what?"

"Here."

"You're...leaving?"

"Yes."

Well, damn. Being in better control than she, he looked around until he saw the front door. He asked, "Are you sure?"

"I told you that you were not to lure me."

She got the whole sentence out. She was recovering. He was disgruntled.

She wobbled over to the door and fumbled with it.

Again he questioned in a fairly ragged voice, "Are you sure?"

Not looking at him, she whispered, "I think so."

He was intense. "Let's talk."

She shook her bowed head and continued trying to open the door.

He smoothed his hair with both hands and, taking deep breaths, he looked at the ceiling for a while. Then he solved the problem of the door for her.

She said quietly, carefully as if talking to some chancy beast, "Help me down the stairs."

He did that, but his hands were a little careless.

She chided him.

He leaned his head down and around to take unfair, sipping kisses.

Her eyes were like saucers. "Don't do that."

At the outside door, he took a deep breath and put his hands into his trouser pockets. He considered her. She was fumbling with the outer door. He allowed that for a minute before he solved that problem also.

She crept out the door and onto the patio. Security sat on one of the benches. Mitch nodded to him and escorted Sally down the access to the street. He walked her to her car. He said, "I'll see you tomorrow."

She nodded, fumbling then with her car keys.

He asked, "Can you drive all right?"

"I think so."

"Come back to my place."

"I don't dare."

He stood up straight and pushed his arms straight. He removed one hand from his pocket, took her keys and unlocked the car for her.

She said, "Thank you."

"Sally—"

She looked at him with unfocused eyes and smiled blindingly.

He said, "Call me when you get home so that I know you got there okay."

She nodded. Then she got into her car and the car crept away, turned the corner and went from his sight.

It was almost a half hour before she called. She said, "Mitch?"

"Sally."

"I'm home."

"Good."

"Safe and . . . sound."

"Yeah."

"Bye."

"Yeah."

She hung up and slowly so did he. He considered their lovers' conversation. They really didn't speak very well. Their words weren't the magic of sunsets or waterfalls or bird-migrating beauty, they were barely even words. But the *feelings* now were all those things. He closed his eyes against the surge of feeling that deliciously crippled him. Then he went out to jog for some long time again.

The next morning, Edgar and his family underlings requested Mitchell Goalong to come to Mr. Jamison's office. Mitch did that.

"Uh, how are things, Mitch?" Edgar was kind.

"Excellent."

"Did you happen to hear what Miss Yoder did yesterday?"

"Yes. It's a brilliant idea."

"You knew yesterday?"

"Yes." Well, of course it had been after-the-fact but it HAD been "yesterday" that he'd heard.

"We were surprised."

"Why?" Mitch's attention was polite.

"It seemed . . . tacky."

"It could have been," Mitch agreed. "But you did notice the skill with which she placed the items? She has an excellent eye. It was well done. I hope she doesn't take one of those many job opportunities she's been offered."

"Ahhh. Well." Edgar Jamison was stymied.

Mitch waited politely. "You have a gem in Miss Yoder. I believe she should have a raise."

The Jamisons all blinked.

Mitch continued, "The items might be changed each day, including different departments. In this land of television hype, Miss Yoder's instant-clarification idea was really excellent."

They were still careful. "Uh . . . yes."

Mitch asked courteously, "Is there anything else?"

"No," said the senior Jamison. "No, no. Thank you for coming to clarify this situation."

"It's my job." He smiled. "Any time." He rose. "Gentlemen." He nodded, smiled and left the windowed office.

So that night at the kitchen table, eating from the Fourth's picnic leftovers, Sally watched Mitch as she said, "Today the Jamisons called me to Edgar's office. I get a raise in pay."

"Good."

"How did you work that?"

"Simple. I explained your display was a good idea."

"They said you recommended the raise."

"Yes."

"Why?"

"It *was* and IS a good idea. You're worth your weight in gold."

She was primly, prissily sassy. "I'll put on a couple more pounds."

They ate the wicked baked beans laced with pork and brown sugar, molasses and vinegar. They had a salad that hadn't even been considered for the picnic. They had Boston brown bread with raspberry jam and they had cottage cheese. They drank a refreshingly dry wine.

She said, "Mitch, you are an unusual man."

"Why?"

"You'll make a great leader."

"Doing what?"

"Anything. You are special."

"How do you mean?"

"You solve things and help other people. You stick your neck out and you're brave."

He smiled.

Very seriously she told him, "You are really something."

His voice roughened as he replied, "So are you."

His morale had soared, his heart melted, his ego expanded. No wonder men in love had such a tough time. Just the physical strain was enough, but all the other parts of a man were affected, their emotions and egos and self-images. It was complicated.

Soooo. He was "in love" with this magical bee?

He said, "I understand the drone that flies highest and gets the queen bee then dies."

"I'm not a bee and you're no drone. A drone is idle and only gears up to impregnate the big, fat queen."

He licked his lips. "You said you were going to put on some weight."

She looked innocently surprised. "You want to impregnate me?"

Earnestly, he urged, "I need to practice . . . first."

She chuckled so deliciously. Her eyes danced and her cheeks pinkened.

How could he have ever thought that she was ordinary?

When she blotted her lips on one of the picnic napkins, he watched. As she rose from her chair, he moved it back for her as he left his own chair. They straightened carefully and, by golly, they were facing one another, their bodies close, their breaths quickening. How had that happened?

And he kissed her. He kissed her long and marvelously and wondrously. She clung and he rubbed his hand on her waist, holding her closer . . . and she burped.

They tried not to, but they couldn't not laugh. Their eyes danced as their closemouthed laughter was shared and that only triggered worse hilarity. It was ridiculous. No burp was that funny.

But their kiss had been so serious, so hungry, so stunning, and a burp is such a common thing.

She said, "I beg your pardon."

"I shouldn't have let you have that last bean."

That set them off again.

"Do you suppose I love you?" He watched her.

"Surely not."

"Why not?" He frowned at her.

"I wouldn't be good for you. I might ruin your career."

"What about my life? If you couldn't love me, it would harm my life's growth."

"No. You are so strong that you can conquer anything and survive anything. You are very sensitive, so you might think you could be harmed, but you would grow on past anything bad in your life. You already have. Your life hasn't been ordinary."

"I've been lucky with the people who have helped me."

"I wish your mother could have known you. How old were you when she died?"

"Fifteen."

"I wish that she could have seen you then. What were you like?"

"Struggling to dominate in the Brown conglomerate of siblings."

"And you won a place."

"I'm not sure anyone noticed my place."

"From the need to dominate, how did you get to this wider view of people, the tolerance you have, the compassion?"

"I'm not aware of having those talents."

"You demonstrate them daily."

He asked, "How?"

"The guy in the mail room. You told him you needed him. He feels he's your right-hand man."

He was the one who'd funneled Sally's volume of mail through Mitch's office. Mitch responded, "In the mail room, he is."

"But you gave him that feeling."

"How do I make you feel?"

"I haven't been fired. I've been a problem for the Jamisons for over six months. They'd been stretched to their limit when you arrived. Without you, I'd be hunting a job."

"Checking through all those offers you've filed away."

"Against a rainy day," she added.

"Would you leave Fort Wayne?"

"Not right now." She tilted her head to one side as she almost smiled, and she quoted him, "I need to be more than a one-trick pony."

He put his hand around her throat, his thumb tilting her head so that her mouth was closer. He growled, "You're full of tricks." And he kissed her.

The whole room exploded with their passion. Waterfalls roared down one wall, the sunset was blinding to the east...west...wherever, and the migrating birds made a hell of a racket.

They separated, raggedly, and he leaned his hands on the table, supporting himself, while she put her hands into her own hair and tried for reorientation.

He managed the words, "You're killing me."

"I don't know what it is about you. I've kissed men be—"

"Who?"

"—fore and it's never been this shattering! You are dangerous for a woman. Why can't you just kiss nicely? Why do you have to shake me up and turn me inside out?"

"I'm an innocent man."

She stared at him in shocked disbelief. She made a rather rude sound of rejection. She said, "Balderdash!" She picked up her purse and walked out.

How had she managed to walk straight to the front door?

Seven

With Sally walking out of his apartment that way, Mitch had to get himself organized and under control so that he could at least see her to her car. He took some deep breaths and looked around.

The kitchen was intact. That was strange. And the dishes were still on the table. Sally hadn't done her share of the cleanup.

Moving stiffly, Mitch aimed for the door and went out, leaving it open, and checked to be sure his front-door key was in his pocket. It was. He went to the stairs, which were fortunately downward. He wasn't sure he'd be able to climb stairs for a while.

He got out the front door and glanced at security who pointed in the other direction. Mitch followed that way and caught up with the Terror who was Sally Yoder. He said, "You didn't do your share in the kitchen."

She asked suspiciously, "My share . . . of what?"

"Cleaning up!" He was indignant.

"I'll do double duty tomorrow. I cook and clean up."

"I can accept that."

"Just don't make a habit of it. How did you know I hadn't helped clean up?"

"It's all still on the table."

She stopped walking. "You could look around and evaluate that?" She was irritated.

"How did you manage to walk straight to the front door?"

She continued walking. "I don't know."

"Where are we going?"

"I've forgotten where I parked my car."

"How far did you walk to get to my place?"

"Not far."

"Then your car should be reasonably close. We'll circle around."

"How can you 'circle' with square blocks?"

"God, but you're a stickler."

"I know."

"Do you have other flaws?"

"My opinion? Or criticism from others?"

He said, "Uh-oh."

"You're coming out of it?"

"Out of what?"

"Whatever it is that happens to my brain cells when you kiss me."

"So you are aware that we are pretty cosmic kissers. I don't believe I have anything to do with it. I've never experienced such a reaction in my brain before this, so it has to be you."

Somewhat terse, she warned, "Don't try to weasel out of the responsibility."

"Why is it my fault? All I do is kiss you and something remarkable happens to the universe. Do you know this last time that the kitchen exploded, a waterfall came down from the roof, the sun set over thataway and birds were singing?"

She gasped. "For you, too?"

"We have a serious problem here."

She said with a hollow voice, "There's an easy solution."

"I hesitate to ask."

In a sorrowful voice, she declared, "Quit kissing. We don't do badly if we don't touch."

"I suppose we could try."

"Yes."

"Wasn't that your car?"

"Where?"

He pointed back several cars.

"Yes. You do distract me. No more kissing."

"Yeah. That's what you say... now."

"I am capable of control."

He made a really very rude sound of disbelief.

She said, "I will see you tomorrow after work, here at your apartment. I shall do the cooking and the cleanup."

"I have taped that declaration."

"I suspected you were that type."

They had come to her car. He said, "Last night when you left, I worried if you would get home all right."

"I was a zombie."

"Good night, Sally."

"Night."

And he leaned over and kissed her smack on the mouth and ruined EVERYTHING.

She gasped and gestured and held her head, and he leaned soberly against her car and just watched, not able to do anything.

She fumbled with the door and he had to organize himself to open it for her. Then she couldn't find her keys and searched everywhere. She did that switching the keys from one hand to clear the other hand for searching.

He took the keys from her hand and selected the ignition key, handing it to her.

She said, "You dirty rat." But she wasn't a good imitator so she didn't sound at all like James Cagney, she just sounded irritated.

She got into her car and slowly drove away like a half-blind new driver, double-checking direction and traffic and she went from his sight.

He stared at the corner where she'd disappeared. Then he looked around and wandered about until he got his bearings. He went back to his apartment and managed to climb the stairs fairly well. He considered that, as she got out of his range, he could function. How far did she have to be from him before he could operate at normal? What was normal?

He made short work of the kitchen, checking the time. Then he called her. She picked up the phone and said, "I'm here, no thanks to you, you lecher."

He disguised his voice and asked, "Mary Lou?"

She hung up.

He dialed again.

She picked up the phone and said in a terrible, lousy, thick drawl, "Rhett, honey, you straighten yourself out." And she hung up.

He went out and ran for miles. When he returned home, he showered. Then going into his room, he opened the closet door to look at his love. Was this lust or love? He pondered that.

But he went to bed and his dreams were filled with wanting.

The next night Mitch was eagerly there, waiting on the patio. He smiled at her nicely and opened the door for her. She said, "Keep your distance."

He stood around watching her busily washing her hands at the sink, getting ready to fix his supper. She began to take things from his refrigerator.

He said, "Here's a key to the front door downstairs and to this place. In case you get here first tomorrow."

"Oh. That's considerate. Put it on my purse."

She didn't offer him a key to her place in exchange. But he had given her his. That gave him an unduly strong feeling of satisfaction. Was it because she had a key to his place? He'd figure it out later.

His hands were in his pockets as he kept shifting and taking steps. He didn't say a word.

She stopped once and said, "If you ever expect to eat, go into the other room!"

"I haven't said anything! And I haven't begun to touch you!"

"Now, Mitch—"

"Yeah...NOW!" And he grabbed her. She gasped so her mouth was open and vulnerable, and the kiss was devastating. Who ever realized that romance authors actually knew what they were writing about? But...who would have thought Fort Wayne, Indiana, would be the center of an 11.7 earthquake!

He crushed her to him and put his arms over her head to protect her from the falling roof. And all was still.

He looked at her wide eyes.

She asked cautiously, "An earthquake?"

He wouldn't release her, so he shrugged a little in the helplessness of it. "Just . . . us."

Her big eyes moved as she checked out the ceiling. "How will we ever know if it's real or if it's just . . . us?"

"There has to be a subtle difference. We'll have to experiment."

"Doing . . . what?"

He shrugged again. "Hugging . . . kissing."

"We could get a seismograph."

His voice was doubtful and slow. "We'd probably spin it off the top of its capability. We'd have to keep getting new ones." He still didn't ease his arms from their tight clench of her. "I believe we simply have to do this a good deal . . . and get used to each other. I believe in the old saying of longtime friends being easy with one another. Since you want to avoid getting too involved, for now, then the only thing to do is to hug and kiss and fool around enough so that we can be comfortable together."

"You could sell a refrigerator to an Eskimo."

"How am I doing with you?"

"I did hear your premise, but I do know you. You're smooth and sly and you like kissing me. You're willing to put up with the whole chaotic mess because you like kissing me."

He pushed his lower lip out as if to pout, and considered the view from the kitchen window. "It's more than that. I like your body. I'm working on getting you out of your clothes."

"Oh." She said that as if it hadn't been something she knew. "You really ARE a lecher!"

"Yeah." He nodded three or four times in little bobs, his face serious and he expanded on it, "I want to fool around with you."

"You want to rub me and see—"

"You got it."

"—if you can make me burp again."

And he laughed. He really laughed. He hugged her tighter, which had to be a miracle, considering how he was clutching her as it was, and he rocked her a little as he laughed.

"You have to let me go. I have so much to do to-night."

Naturally he inquired, "What?"

"I have to watch some tapes. I've promised."

His arms reluctantly, minimally loosened. "What sort of tapes?"

"I don't know yet."

"Double X rated?"

"Just see how your mind works!"

"Well, I just thought I might help."

"Thanks anyway. Let me go. I must get supper on the table. Good grief, look at the time!"

"How can you possibly focus on the clock?" He was disgruntled so he kissed her again.

She did struggle and make sounds for almost five seconds before she cooperated and then began making little moves and soft hungry sounds and breathing oddly and driving him berserk.

For supper, they had rushed peanut-butter sandwiches and milk, with bananas for dessert. Her clothes
were askew, her hair a mess.

His eyes were hot on her. "You can't go off and
leave me in this condition." He was firm.

"I didn't do anything! It's your problem."

"I never had this problem before in all my life."

"Hah!"

"You have no heart."

"Right."

She put the paper plates in the recycling basket,
wiped off the table and said, "There."

"Where?"

"Good night. Supper was unusual."

"You're hard-hearted."

She laughed. "It's a good thing."

"What about me?"

"Poor Mitch. It's your own fault. You should have
left me alone."

"You kissed back."

"You're a marvelous kisser."

"How many men have you kissed?"

"None to compare to you. All the rest were so
pleasant. No earthquakes, no wickedness...not nearly
so delicious. But really nice."

"You liked mine."

"I'm leaving."

"Don't go. Stay with me."

"No. Sex isn't something you do just because it feels
good."

He gasped. "You're a virgin!"

She got huffy. "It's very apparent to me that you
are not!"

He smiled. "You've never made love with anyone else."

"Not with anyone," she corrected.

"You must be the last one over twenty-one on this whole entire planet."

She looked down her nose at him. "You've been checking?"

"You're in for a treat."

"Has that line been a zinger?"

He laughed.

"How do I know you're not riddled with all the minor diseases, not counting the fatal one?"

"On my honor. And you?"

"As you've guessed, I'm pure."

He grinned. "Pure enough for now."

"I'm going home."

"Please stay. I promise I won't do anything more than you want me to do."

She turned her head as if trying to locate a sound. "That has a very familiar ring. You guys all taught that in gym at school? At the pool hall?"

"Who's said that to you?"

"It's one of the sayings quoted at slumber parties."

"In high school?"

"Women share. That's why most of us aren't caught unaware."

"I really meant it. I don't want you to leave. If you'll just talk to me and let me watch you, that'll be enough. I believe you're a miracle. You saw the picture in my closet. I—"

"I've been meaning to ask you about that. Why...in the closet? Are you ashamed of me?"

He said, "Come look."

He took her into the entrance hall and opened the closet door. He took out the second picture and put it on the empty picture hook on the wall. "That was so you could greet me when I came home."

"Another closet."

"I didn't think you'd understand if you walked in here and saw that blown-up newspaper picture right there. I was afraid you'd think I was weird."

She was blushing just a little with her pleasure and she tightened her smile to minimize it. "Probably. I've not seen much to recommend— No. I can't say that. I've already told you that you're a very remarkable man. You are. You scare me. I'm so susceptible to you that I'm afraid. Is this real? Or am I being lured into a sexual clash that would devastate me? I'm trying to be careful of myself. For myself."

"I'll take care of you." He was sober and watched her seriously.

They looked at each other for a serious time, then she said, "Please, Mitch, don't tempt me so. I must go home."

He looked down. "You are committed to coming to supper tomorrow."

"Yes."

Then he said, "I'll walk you down."

As emotionally charged as they were, they didn't speak again. Not until they got to her car. She didn't even try, but just handed him the keys. He unlocked and opened the car door, and he sorted the ignition key, giving it to her.

Then he kissed her.

They were on the street. The traffic was light. But he didn't give her a double-whammy devastating kiss. No. He curled forward from his waist, tilted his head and only touched her mouth with his. He gave her a sweet salute that exploded skyrockets and melted her bones. So, yet again, she drove away with extreme care, watching corners and traffic and lights.

With the needed time passed, he called her. "You're there?"

"By the skin of my teeth."

Alarmed, he asked, "What happened?"

"You." And she hung up softly.

What with one thing and another, jogging and all, he should have slept that night, but he did not.

The next morning Mitch went to work and all the women just about swooned over him. He looked like a green-eyed young Laurence Olivier playing Heathcliff, smoldering and anguished.

Everyone was particularly kind to him. He didn't notice that he was especially considerate in a distracted way. His eyes rested on Rembrandt's windmill under the lowering sky. He was that windmill, big, solid, immobile, waiting for the winds of Sally to turn him and make him move and come alive.

Searching for her in order to look at her to reassure himself that she was real, Mitch went through the store. He found no sign of her. How could that be? She was always one place or another, interfering.

She wasn't there. At least not that he could determine without asking everyone or calling her over the intercom. He couldn't do that. He would see her that evening. He ate a scant lunch with indifference and walked outside around the parking lot for a while.

Mitch had a call that afternoon that the bronzed, used cigar was ready. Mitch hung up the phone, told his shared secretary that he had an errand and would be back in a half hour. He went out and got the plaque. It was wrapped in brown paper and tied with a thick string. He took it up to his apartment and laid it, still wrapped, on the kitchen table.

He went back to work and managed not to louse up anything the rest of the afternoon.

Mitch left the store just a little early. He wanted to be there when she arrived. He wanted her to use his key to open the doors. It filled him to think of her having access to him.

So he had a while to pace around and fidget. Her picture was back up in the front hall now, quite openly. He would stop and study her. Then he'd move around again, looking critically at his apartment. It wasn't yet a home. It was static when she wasn't there to make the air electric.

The doorbell rang downstairs and Mitch frowned. She'd lost the key? Had she forgotten she had it? He went to the speaker and said, "That you?"

And it was Pike!

Pike laughed and said, "Probably not who you're expectin'. I doubt you're free this evening?"

"That's right."

"Are we going to chat this way, or can I come up?"

"Uh—"

"I can sit down here on the patio and wait until whoever it is comes along," he offered cheerfully. "Anyone I know?"

"God, Pike, you're intruding. Come on up. But make it quick."

"Sure. I understand."

Mitch punched the release, and Pike took the stairs a puffing two at a time. In one chuffing breath, Pike said, "A bunch of us are going up to one of the lakes

Sunday. We've rented a pontoon and we're all bringing food and beer and we'll have a blast. Come along and bring your mysterious female visitor.''

"How do you know my visitor is a woman?"

Saying the obvious, Pike replied, "Anyone else, you wouldn't be so touchy."

"Let me check it out, and I'll call you later this evening." He dug out his wallet. "Let me pay my share on the pontoon and beer, so you don't hunt down someone else." He pulled out two bills and proffered them. "Okay? You're nice to ask. It sounds like a great day."

Still standing in the hall, Pike grinned as he selected one bill from Mitch's hand. "It will be. Try to come along. This is a good bunch."

"Thanks, Pike. Sorry to run you off. I will call later."

"Okay. Hope to see you Sunday."

Pike turned away just as Sally came up the stairs carrying a bouquet. Grinning widely he said, "Hi, Sally," as if they met on Mitch's stairs every day.

She was startled and unsettled.

Pike turned back at the landing and called, "If you forget to call tonight, be at my place on Sunday morning about eight. Okay? See you guys later."

And he was gone.

The two lovers stood where they were until they heard the click of the outside door. Then they looked at each other—and Mitch grinned.

"You beast! You set this up to compromise me."

"No."

"I know you didn't. But the cat's out of the bag."

"Pike won't tell that you were here."

"Pike is the telegraph dispatcher of this entire community. He knows everything about everyone."

"So... you came to supper."

In a dead tone she added, "And I have a key to your front door."

He looked aside to try to conceal his pleasure at that... at everyone soon knowing. Sally wore his brand, as of that minute.

"I have supper almost ready. Come on inside. You might as well eat."

"I'm ruined."

"Not yet."

She gave him a cold look that should have shriveled him.

It did not. He was a courteous host. He went to her and took her arm, leading her into his den. Her feet were reluctant.

She had brought a bouquet of zinnias. That pleased him most of all. Pike knew, with the flowers, that this was not a casual visit. She had accepted an invitation, she'd even brought flowers, she had a key to his place... she was compromised.

Everyone would soon know. It could complicate her life. Not his so much, but hers. Maybe not.

He knew he wouldn't try to mend this. He would allow Pike's tongue to share in spreading the word that Sally belonged to Mitch. Would she stand for it?

She'd said, "The cat's out of the bag." While she'd been disgruntled, she hadn't been hand-wringingly appalled. She would rather have kept their outside acquaintance unknown, but she had admitted with those words that it was now no secret they were acquainted enough so that she had a key to his place.

That did make it sound as if they were a couple, not just acquainted or friends, but lovers.

He wished.

He was careful of her, so as not to scare her off any more than she was. He closed his apartment door and turned to smile at her. She wasn't there. She had dropped her purse on a chair and was headed for the kitchen. She was trying to make short shrift of supper and get away?

She was filling the zinnia vase with water and as he watched she took it to the table. The string-tied brown-paper-wrapped plaque was lying in the middle of the table. She picked it up, and he said, "Leave it on the table. It's for you."

She looked at it and then at him. "What is it?"

"It's for dessert."

"It's too heavy for cookies or pie."

"No pinching or squeezing—" he licked his lips "—the package. You have to wait."

For their meal, he had salmon. There was a fresh salad marinated with the dressing. None of the foods had ever even been considered for the July Fourth picnic. She looked at the display of goodies before she turned and looked at him. "We've run out of picnic food."

"There are the weiner rolls."

"You have hard rolls here."

"I love them," he admitted with undue fervency.

"You have lured me here under false pretenses."

He nodded, agreeing.

"You gave me the keys so that Pike could catch me in a compromising position."

"On my honor, I was appalled when Pike came here. I didn't know he would. He invited us to come to a lake on Sunday. A bunch have rented a pontoon boat. It's an all-day affair. Picnic, swimming, drinking beer, laughing, scratching and telling lies.''

''Do you tell lies?'' she asked soberly.

''Only on beer picnics on lakes in summer.'' His own face was serious. ''Come with me. It'll be fun.''

''I'll...see.''

She put the salmon to bake, having dribbled lemon juice on it. When it was done, she sprinkled tiny fresh dill leaves over it and lay a sprig on top of the fish.

Mitch poured the white wine. They sat down, served their salads, and Mitch retrieved the hot hard rolls. They ate silently. The salmon was superb, the salad perfect, the rolls crunchy and the wine was an excellent choice.

She said, ''You are an interesting man.''

''I find you riveting.''

''That's sex.''

He considered that comment. ''I believe sex might well be a part of my riveting interest in you.''

''You admit it!''

''I would hardly kiss someone the way we kiss if my interest was only—interest.''

''How would you kiss 'only interested?' ''

''On the cheek.''

''You've kissed my cheek salaciously.''

He said the obvious, his voice underlining that, ''It was your cheek. Another cheek wouldn't get more than a peck.''

''You've given me pecks. Were those times of friendliness?''

''Those kisses may have seemed like pecks only because they were brief. They shriveled my gizzard and inflamed me in other places." He gave her a steady, straight look.

"Oh."

"You're driving me crazy."

"Because I'm eating salmon?"

"Because you breathe."

She was indignant. "I have to breathe!"

"Your chest moves."

"My lungs are under it." She frowned at him.

"And your breasts jiggle."

"How dare you to notice that!"

"Who can help it? You wear high heels and you take quick steps and . . . you jiggle."

"I'll get an iron corset."

"No."

"I wouldn't . . . jiggle then."

"You'd ruin my day."

"Well," she said elaborately. "We certainly can't do something so rash as to ruin your day!"

She was getting testy. He asked kindly, "Want some lemon yogurt?"

She agreed. "A taste."

"Then you can open your package."

She touched it again. "I can't figure out what it is."

"You'll see."

"You shouldn't buy presents for me."

"I do as I choose."

She looked at him. "I believe that's one of the most honest statements you've made so far. The wiliness of you is that you make your arbitrary actions seem logical."

"Probably."

"I am fascinated by your honesty."

"I'm working on other fascinations. Humor, sex, kindness, sex, courtesy, sex—"

"I figured that out earlier."

He chided, "You didn't kiss me hello."

"I was deciding how I could erase my being on the stairs with your key and Pike knowing."

"You're an independent woman in the current world."

"You have a quick and clever tongue. I should have realized that when you saved my neck that first time. You are nothing short of brilliant."

"Thank you, Miss Yoder."

"May I open the package?"

"Let me pour you a little more wine."

"I've really had enough."

"It's for the toast."

"We're going to toast something?"

"Yes."

He could see that she was more cautious. She moved less freely. He gave her scissors to cut the strings. She did that and opened the brown paper. She frowned. Then she studied the bronzed cigar and the date. Her lips parted. She looked at Mitch and a tear gathered and hovered on her lower eyelid. "Oh, Mitch."

"We drink a toast to a woman with balls. I'm proud of you."

The tear spilled over and tracked down her cheek. She ignored it. She said, "Oh, Mitch," again.

She almost unmanned him. His own eyes misted. He smiled. He lifted his glass. His low, husky voice said, "To you."

Eight

A mush-muscled Sally lifted her own glass and smiled. "To me."

"I couldn't believe you'd take that cigar. It was the quickest impulsive stroke of brilliance I've ever witnessed."

"Thank you."

They sipped the wine.

She looked over at him and admitted. "If you hadn't been there, I never would have done it. I had to look good to you."

He smiled and shook his head. "It's very hard not to take the credit. But you know full well that you've been up to your neck in controversy ever since you showed up at Jamisons. And I bet if we went back to your school days, we'd see growing evidence of the evolution of Sally Yoder to the woman you are. People talk about you. They are awed by you. Not so much because of what you've done but that you've survived. You've been a shot in the arm for liberty, truth and justice."

"All that?"

Formally, he bowed his head once as he smiled. "All that."

She tapped one finger against her lips in great thought. "A statue." She decided that. "Salamander Yoder." She moved out an indicating hand with the palm up. "Carrying a—"

"Salamander?"

"My great-grandmother named me. She was perhaps a little senile at the time. Very old." As he scooped her off her chair very carefully and sat her on his lap, she continued describing the statue. "Carrying a torch." She paused, squinting. "A whole lot like the Statue of Liberty." Then she said decisively, "No book. Breasts covered."

"Darn."

"A glimpse of the ankle and that foot."

"Wow."

"I knew you were a leg man."

He immediately shook his head and lifted his hands palm down, denying he was a leg man. "I'm still deciding. It takes a lot of research. Men become known by their preferences. It becomes a label. A man must choose wisely. You could help in this."

"How c—"

"Glad you volunteered. Strip."

"I don't believe you."

"See? We share in similar problems. I can't believe you either. You need to lead me along and help me to understand you and get to know the real Salamander."

She put her elbow on the table, leaned her head on that hand in order to look at him as she inquired, "Did I make a mistake in allowing you to know that?"

He admitted, "It has blackmail potential."

"You beast."

"But I'm an admiring one. Don't forget that."

"What am I doing on your lap?"

"After you opened your package, you looked as if you might cry and I wanted to comfort you."

"I'm amazed you saved that cigar. And to have had it bronzed! It will be precious to me all the rest of my life, because you admired me. Thank you."

"It was your act that won the award. I had nothing to do with it."

"You backed me. You were new with the company and you stuck your neck out for a rogue."

"Rogues are almost always male." He felt the need to clarify that.

She smiled and lifted her fingers to his hair, combing it back. "I've wanted to do that for a long time. This particular section is noncomforming."

He encouraged, "Touch anything you want."

"That's very open of you."

"I'm a sharing man."

To prove that, he kissed her. It was the expected maelstrom of chaotic disaster. Their bodies were buffeted and their hair flew out, their toes curled inside their shoes and their fingers dug into one another to hold on. But it was the roar in their ears peaking to a crescendo.

They didn't notice until their mouths separated.

They sat, she on his lap, and they gasped and shivered. He mumbled, "There has to be a cure for this debilitating stress."

"Yeah, and I'll bet you have what you think is the solution."

"You know what it can be?"

"I know what *you* think it would be."

"If you have the knowledge to solve something as serious as this, you really ought to share it . . . like a good citizen."

"You think it's sex."

"Oh. Yeah! That might do it. Let's see."

He put his arms under her shoulders and knees and stood up as if he always carried a woman around with him.

"Hold it."

"Some problem?"

"I was just saying what you thought it was between us. I wasn't suggesting anything at all."

"That's okay. I can take it from here."

She laughed at the mental image. "You're a contortionist?"

"Don't get sassy."

As he single-mindedly carried her through the living room and into the small dividing hall, she smoothed his hair back and mentioned, "One of the problems with instant gratification is that sometimes it isn't possible."

"We're alone. No one's around but us."

"I have my period."

He stopped walking. He looked at her. He said, "That's okay."

"No."

"Really. It won't make any difference."

"I'd die of embarrassment."

"No you wouldn't. We'll put a towel under us and it'll be okay."

"How do you know that?"

"Guys share things, too."

"No."

"They really do."

"I mean 'no' I won't. Not now."

"In an hour?"

"Good grief! No. Not for a couple of more days."

"I'm not sure I'll last that long."

"You can. Men do."

He considered her. "It really would be all right."

She shook her head.

He carried her in and lay her on his bed. He countered her efforts to get up as he said, "You can at least lie here and let me look at you on my bed. I've dreamed of you being here. See that pillow? That's yours. I've held it every night since I first laid eyes on you. It's only right for you to put your head on it and let me kiss you a little."

He didn't kiss her just a little, he kissed her a whole lot, even on her mouth. He exhausted her with his nuzzling around and kissing and, with his high emotional state, she became languid. He restrained his passion. His petting became less intense. They lay on their sides together and dozed. Both finally went to sleep, lying there, almost in all their clothing.

Even frustration can be exhausting.

On Saturday they wakened early and she was just a tad disoriented. She inquired, "What am I doing here?"

And he replied, "I am so dispirited, I was—"

"Dispirited?"

"Exactly. I was making love to you and you went to sleep."

She considered and admitted, "That was rude."

"Yes."

"Sorry."

He was kind. "You can make amends."

"Let me guess."

"You get three."

"Breakfast in bed?"

He laughed. Then he decided, "That's part."

"Today's cleaning day?"

"Why... I hadn't even thought of that. It could be part."

She bit her lower lip and looked around elaborately, trying to think of something else. She said, "I give up."

"That's *it!*"

Holding him off, turning her head, she complained, "You even wake up this way? Figuring the angles and being clever? There's something really wrong with someone who wakes up being clever."

"We get ahead."

"Not today you don't. Behave. What am I doing in your bed at 7:14 on a Saturday morning, still in my yesterday's clothes?"

He protested in defensive indignation: "I did try to get you out of them."

"I remember that."

"You were obstinate."

"I'm modest."

"You're beautiful and obstinately modest."

She pulled her blouse down. "Not entirely."

He prevented the rearrangement. "You are simply breathtaking."

"Naw. I'm just like all the others."

"Is that right?"

"Come on, Mitchell, don't try to hornswoggle me."

"Hornswoggle?"

"Fool?"

"You want to fool around?"

"No! Cut that out!"

"You are so selfish." He was disgusted, but his eyes were filled with laughter and his lips quirked. He said, "Let's see if my beard is the right kind."

"For... what?"

"For whiskering. For rubbing in your neck and along your arms." He moved slowly, putting a hand on the other side of her, lifting his chest to lie on top of hers.

"What?" She watched him with amused caution. "What are you trying now?"

"This. Hold still. Now, Sally! How can I do this if you don't hold still? There. Now lift your chin. There... how's... that."

"Ohhhhh."

"Like that?"

"That's wicked."

"Our foster mother loved our dad doing that to her. When we were little we all jumped around them and demanded that he do us too. Gives you goose bumps, doesn't it?"

"Ummmmm."

"Want some more?" His throat clacked with his slow words.

"Better not."

"You have to know it would be all right."

"Not now." She was sober. But she lifted her hand to his softly rough cheek and she was gentle.

His green eyes looked down into her blue ones. He smiled just a little. "Uh—about breakfast in bed, lie still and I'll bring you anything you want."

"My purse."

He was expansive. "You don't have to pay, you know. This bed-and-breakfast is free."

"No. I have to... freshen up."

"It just so happens I have indoor plumbing, hot and cold running water, shampoo and all the frills."

She slanted a look at him. "Women's clothing?"

"My robe?"

"That's pretty good."

"And I still have those jogging trousers you used. They're clean again, and I have an extensive selection in T-shirts."

"I accept."

"Uh... that was the 'universal' acceptance, and I *have* made other offers, so—"

"The shower, the robe, the jogging trousers, the—"

"Oh, *that* sort of acceptance." He wilted a little. "I thought you were accepting me."

"You're really very dramatic." She sat up lazily and stretched discreetly.

Watching her distractedly, Mitch said, "You'll have to meet Felicia."

Cautiously Sally inquired, "Is she your foster mother? I seem to recall your mentioning her?"

"Yep. Nobody can hold a candle to her for dramatics. She's something."

Sally straightened and turned her head, her glance downward.

"You hostile about something?"

"Of course not. I need a shower."

He smiled. "This way, my lady."

He took her hand and helped her step down from the bed as he watched. He led her to the bathroom and showed her the linen closet and the supply of soap and his robe hanging on the back of the door. He said, "I'm especially good at scrubbing places you can't reach."

"Had a lot of practice?"

He laughed. "You're quick and—suspicious! No. I was responsible for one of the dogs at home. I'm especially good with flea soap."

"I do not have fleas."

"Prevention is the greater part of valor."

"That's 'honor.' "

"I am."

"Honor is the better part of valor."

"I'm honorable."

"And flealess?"

"No parasites."

She ignored his flippancy and just watched him, quite seriously. "You really are honorable."

"I believe I love you."

"You couldn't possibly." Her voice was a little breathless. She couldn't seem to exhale.

"I can remember sometimes asking my dad and the other guys that lived at the Browns, how does a guy know? And they all said, 'You'll know.' "

"I need the shower."

"You don't want to hear about this?"

"I think you're building up to kiss me again and I need a shower."

"Sometimes a little sweat can be erotic."

"Then I *really* need a shower."

"You're avoiding the issue."

She laughed.

"No issue. I have condoms."

She stopped pushing him toward the bathroom door and asked, "Why?"

"I got them Tuesday." That wasn't true, but it sounded better.

"You thought I was coming here for supper in order to seduce you?"

He gave her a tender smile. "Or the other way around. I really just wanted to be ready for you."

"Let me see the box."

"You want to see the *box?* Why would you want to see the box? Do you prefer a particular kind? I thought you said—"

"I want to see if you've opened it."

He laughed. She was very clever. An old battered box about a third full? He said, "It isn't full. I've been practicing so I could be smooth for you."

She looked around. "Where's the box?"

"In good time. Don't get me excited. I'm having a hard enough time as it is." He bent his head with excessively poignant suffering.

She said, "Bah!"

He complained, "Sadistically stolid Salamander Yoder!"

She put her hands into her hair. "My God, just listen to that! I should *never* have told you that! I'll be hearing that from you all the rest of my life!"

Smooth as silk, he purred, "So you're going to hang around my neck? You're taken with me?"

"Not in the least! You beast! You're just the type who'll tell everyone that name and it will spread all through the Allen County area and I'll *never* hear the last of it!"

"It really has a nice ring to it. 'Salamander Yoder for president.' Not bad. 'Salamander Yoder makes World News Network yet again. The station's owner considers putting Salamander Yoder on retainer as newsworthy.' Probably."

"Go cook breakfast."

He grinned at her. "I like having you here at my place. Move in."

She looked at him in shock. "You're leading me down the primrose path to degradation! I was caught coming into your place with your key in my hand, and now I've spent the night. What's happening to me?"

"Not enough."

"You have a one-track mind."

"My mind isn't too bad, it's my body that's giving me trouble."

"Control is the answer."

"I'm trying, but you don't cooperate."

"Control of yourself!"

"Ohhhh. I hadn't understood that premise at all. I thought—"

"Go." She enunciated carefully. "Go to the kitchen and fix us something to eat."

"You use my shower, my clothes, my bed, and now you want me to feed you! What do I get out of all this?"

"Respect."

He laughed and went out the door, which she immediately shut and locked.

Through the door, he said, "Oh, Sally, I forgot to tell you. Don't lock the door. The lock sticks and we'd have to get the locksmith to open it again."

She gasped and turned the lock, and it worked.

He opened the door and smiled. "Coffee right away."

She closed and locked the door.

She stripped and turned on the shower. She got in and scrubbed and stood in the hot spray and relished it. She washed her hair and washed it again and she felt like a new woman. The bathroom filled with steam, but it quickly lessened.

She got out, dried herself and looked for his deodorant. Anything was better than nothing. And there on the lavatory counter was a hot cup of coffee!

She stared at it and tried the door. It was locked. She looked around. It was the only door. He had a key.

She put on his robe, dried her hair and fluffed it. She put on enough makeup to look like a living person, then she marched into the kitchen to mention a gentleman never opens locked doors uninvi—

There was a note. It read:

There are squishy sugared doughnut holes, a hard-boiled egg and more coffee. Edgar called for a consultation. I'll be back at noon. I love having you...in my bed.

M.G.

Now how was she to keep a salacious sounding note like that? She folded it and put it into her purse. She sat down and ate her allotted share. He'd had the gall to count them and split them exactly. He'd probably had a third of them and halved the rest of them so that she would think she'd gotten her share. They were delicious.

The hard-boiled egg was . . . different for breakfast, but okay. And he really made a good cup of coffee. She walked around with her second cup, opening drawers and checking things out. In one drawer, she discovered her model's panties. Sally touched them, thoughtfully sober, but she left them there.

She didn't find any condoms anywhere. He must have a secret hiding place? She made an earnest search and found the videotape. "S.Y." She smiled at it.

Sally put on his jogging trousers and one of his T-shirts. She rolled up her discarded clothing and she printed a note that said, "Thank you for your hospitality. S.Y." Then wearing her heels from yesterday and carrying her bundle of clothing, she left the apartment and went down to her car. It was not there.

It was Saturday. It had been at a parking meter that charges nothing after-hours. That morning, it had been towed?

She called the police. They didn't know anything about her car. They had not towed such a car. If she wanted to file a stolen-car report, she would have to come down to the police station.

She said, "One of my family might have removed it. I'll let you know if they didn't and come file a report." She called Mitch at Jamisons.

His shared secretary said, "I'm sorry. Mr. Goalong is in a meeting. May I take a message?"

"No. Thank you. I'll call later."

"I'll tell him you called, Sally."

That was stunning. The shared secretary had recognized her voice! Sally said, "Thank you. It wasn't important."

Her car had been out on that street all alone, all night long. Whatever could have happened to it? And look at her. Dressed as she was, she was going to take a cab, go home and get out of it and walk into her half of the house in broad daylight? Scandalous.

In the bottom of her purse, she found a slender silk scarf that unfolded miraculously into a very generous square. She put her cast-off clothing into that and tied it at the top like a hobo's carryall.

Then in the cab she took off her shoes. Heels with jogging pants made her look strange. She stuck those into her bag.

She paid before she left the cab and got out of it with élan. She walked up to her door and two neighbors called to her. She waved without stopping.

She got inside as if she'd made home base after a scavenger hunt. She changed into her own clothing and distractedly did her Saturday chores.

Mitch called her right at noon and asked, "Why did you leave?"

She guessed, "You noticed I didn't do your cleaning?"

"I have a lady who comes every other Tuesday. Why didn't you wait for me?"

"I needed to get home. My car's missing."

"No, it isn't. I put it in the parking garage last night."

"You got up in the night and moved my car?"

"Sure. I didn't want it towed. How'd you get home?"

"A taxi."

"I'm sorry, honey."

"No problem."

"I'll bring your car out and you can take me back. Okay?"

"When?"

"Now? Do you have peanut butter? I recall you making me a terrific peanut-butter sandwich. With milk. And a banana."

"I believe I can oblige."

"How far does your obliging go?"

"Not past a sandwich, milk and a banana."

"Frugal."

She smiled at the phone, since he couldn't see her. "When will you arrive? I want the sandwich to be fresh for you."

"And you're thoughtful. How about now?"

"I can handle that."

"I need to be kissed."

"Uh-oh. That again."

"Yeah. Practice puckering up."

"I just—"

But he'd hung up.

She found she paced, waiting for him. She made the sandwiches in short order, adding cheese, tomatoes, crisp bacon, lettuce and mayonnaise. She had fresh chips and she put the glasses of milk back into the refrigerator.

Her car came into the driveway and he stopped it. He got out and looked around as he always did. He came up onto her porch as she opened her door to invite him into her cooled house. He came inside, smiled at her and opened his arms.

She closed the door and walked right into his arms, against his body and put her eager lips up for his.

And he kissed her.

One hell of a tornado hit right then. The house shook and wobbled and spun. The sounds roared in high volume and the windows shivered and rattled.

He gradually drew his mouth away and she saw how serious he was. He said, "It wasn't my imagination."

She didn't care what wasn't his imagination. In the still silence, she lifted her mouth again.

They went on fooling with the stability of the universe and toying with the balance of the earth for some time. They weren't the least concerned with whatever havoc they were tempting there. They just tried to get closer and closer, pressing their straining bodies against each other while they tried to breathe through their ears.

He lifted his mouth to say, "I wanted you at my place when I got there." The apartment had been empty and static again. He'd felt abandoned. Just that stiff little note was there to greet him.

"Are you hungry?"

He went back to hugging her and he made hungry sounds.

She wiggled until he reluctantly released her. She took his hand and led him to the lavatory so that he could wash, then she led him to the table. She served him. And he ate.

Mitch took his first bite and chewed thoughtfully. Then he peeked between the pieces of bread to see what he was eating.

She covered it with her hand and said, "Guess."

"Bacon and tomato? Peanut butter. And cheese? Lettuce. It's an interesting combination."

"It's a good, balanced sandwich."

So he had to see if it would, indeed, balance.

When they'd reassembled that half, they laughed. Everything was interesting or amusing. He had another sandwich. He sat back. He stretched and yawned hugely and said, "I have to have a nap." He looked at her with such restrained humor. "You slept in my bed last night. It's only fair I get to nap in yours."

She gave him a superior glance. "I have a guest room."

"So do I, but I'm friendlier than you. I shared my bed. Now you have to share yours."

She took him upstairs and showed him her room. He walked around, looking at her things. He took off his suit jacket and handed it to her to be hung up. He removed his tie, then his shoes and socks.

His shirt was unbuttoned. He gave her his arms so that she unbuttoned his cuffs. She helped him to remove the shirt and she put the shirt on a hanger, straightening it. She hung it away.

She was watching soberly as he emptied his trouser pockets and lay his things on her dresser. Then he unbuttoned his trousers and unzipped them.

He glanced up and saw that she was watching. He slid them off his hips with a little trouble. He explained, "I've been that way since I first saw you."

She was silent.

"Do I scare you?"

She shook her head a little.

"I have great control." He placed the legs of the pants together and shook them out. She gave him a hanger and he put them on it.

He said, "Come. We need the rest. We're going dancing tonight. I want to spend the night holding you again and that's the safest way, in public. But somehow I'm just a little sleepy. Try to keep your hands off me for an hour or so."

They got into her bed from either side and met in the middle. He gave her a careful kiss, sighed hugely, put his arms around her and pulled her close to him.

He made a purring sound in his throat. He lay quietly. He said, "Try not to wiggle and I'll pretend you're the pillow."

She lay still and said nothing.

He sighed a couple of times and settled a little differently. Then he sighed differently. And he slept.

Sally lay awake.

Nine

___

Mitch fell asleep so quickly. Sally put her hand beneath her cheek on her pillow and watched him. How could he have such a clear conscience—being in a strange woman's bed, that way—and sleep so heavily? Was she going to allow this rash and quick freedom to continue? Where was she going to call a halt? Or was she?

And she wondered how he could so easily have weaseled his way into her life. He didn't appear to be as practiced as he must be.

How many women had he snookered into spending the night with him? She couldn't believe that she'd actually done that. And here he was in her bed. She'd certainly never intended allowing that.

He gave her such confidence that she was safe and in charge of him. He was either sincere or he was very crafty and dangerous.

He was so open with her. She needed to take him to meet her parents. She would watch her dad the entire time. He was a man who appeared nonjudgmental, but Sally knew him too well and she could always tell what he thought. They were alike.

What would her dad think of Mitch? She quietly, quietly lifted his arm from over her stomach and slid from the bed. She walked barefooted across the room. She carefully, carefully closed the door after her.

And in the bed Mitch's eyes slitted open and he smiled a little. He settled more comfortably and then he did actually, gradually go to sleep.

Sally tiptoed downstairs and called her sister, Betty. "You remember the Fourth, when I canceled?"

"Yeah."

"How about going to Kaboom's tonight and meeting the reason?"

"Oh?"

"Yeah, but golly, I don't know." She dug her fingers into her hair. "This scares me a little. It's been so—fast."

"Are you—?"

"Of course not! Really, Betty."

"You realize the Cubs play baseball this afternoon? You know how involved Ralph gets? He'll be recovering this evening. This will take a lot of maneuvering. Do you understand what all I will have to do? You'll owe me all sorts of Brownie points, but I will manage to be there."

"And Ralph. I value his opinion."

"Sure. And I'll get Pop and Mom and the rest of the siblings. Hush. And our shriveled up little old greatgranny from the home. Do you know what she really named John? You don't want to know. We'll ALL be there.... Be quiet. You're supposed to be listening. And we'll all stand around and stare."

"Forget I called."

"Hey, this is serious?"

"Oh, Betty—"

"Hmmm. I'll get Joe and Tiny."

"Maybe not. Brothers can get peculiar around potentials."

"So he's a ... potential?"

"What do you think this is all about?"

"It would help to know his name."

"Mitchell Goalong. Go ahead and make a crack."

"Elbedia Yoder would comment on a name?"

"Yeah. He knows I'm Salamander."

"You've already told him *that?*"

"I haven't showed him my scars and moles as yet."

"I see. Well, honey, some of us will—accidentally and with GREAT surprise—be there. I'll screen them carefully. I promise. You did a great job in my struggle to get Ralph."

"He's a fascinating animal. He thinks men rule."

"Little child, they do."

After Betty had said goodbye, Sally sat there for some time, then she emerged from her fog, quickly looked at her watch, got up, went into the living room and turned on the TV. She sorted out a tape for the VCR, put a pad and pencil on her sewing table and began to work.

The film was science fiction and it was earnestly done. It was one she could watch without discipline, and time passed.

As the creature lifted the heroine up to dash her against the purple rocks indigenous to that planet, Mitch came into the room. He was still in his B.V.D.s and looked as if he could handle the beast all by himself. She said, "Shhh. This is the end."

He sat down and leaned back to watch. The rocket came from one side, blasting away the creature's clawed appendage, and instantly shot a towline into the severed bit, which still clung around the heroine. The day was saved. And the blonde heroine also.

The end.

As the tape rewound, Mitch leaned forward a little so that he could turn and look at Sally full-face. "There are aspects to you that I hadn't realized."

She was hard put not to laugh. He thought she'd chosen to watch that film? She replied, "I am the arbitrator who judges and recommends the videotapes for sale at Jamisons. People need to know what to expect."

He thought how typical of her to sew while she was watching something. Her Busy-Bee syndrome was woven throughout her life. Carefully he inquired, "How will you rate that one?"

"Action/innovative/adventure. Not *Star Wars*."

"Yeah." He sat back slowly and stared at the blank screen.

She offered, "The next one is a remake of *Camille*—"

"Ugh."

"You've seen it?"

"Who wants to go through all that with them?"

He'd betrayed himself. His emotions could be caught by a film. She said, "Actually, that isn't next. It's a comedy. Would you like to see part? We have the time."

"Time?"

"We're going to dinner and dancing. You promised. You needed a nap so that you could dance with me tonight. You have talent that must not be idle."

"I have other—"

"Never mind."

"Easy for you to say."

She raised her eyebrows prissily and tightened her mouth. "So you're actually a one-trick pony...too?"

And he laughed. He tried to stop as he looked at her, but he just laughed. She finally had to also. His laughter was so infectious. His eyes were so wickedly naughty.

She gave him iced tea and some cookies she'd made. Later she shared an apple, banana and orange. And she saw to it that he drank enough water. She was taking care of him.

After the comedy ended, he asked, "How will you rate that?"

"It probably should be seen in a group. Laughter sometimes must be shared. To watch a comedy alone takes clever writing and a skilled performance. It's the words more than the visual for a single viewer. Otherwise it just looks as if it's reaching blindly."

He nodded as she spoke, agreeing, then he asked, "How will you state your advice about that one?"

"Group/beer/tolerance."

"How did you come to do this?"

"Customers tried to return tapes. You know that. So to protect ourselves, we have to screen them."

"Who else does this?"

"I do it."

"As time-consuming as it must be, it can't be that exciting."

"Some of the unknown films are gems. Some of the known ones are terrible. All hype. If someone is going to spend around twenty bucks, they ought to know what they're buying."

"So you view them all?"

"We tried other people, but they weren't neutral. The films were okay or good or awful. We needed someone who could distance themselves in order to be honest and neutral."

"How do you stand it?"

"I sew."

"What do you . . . sew."

"I make my own clothes."

He grinned. "And you told me that you had to eat at my house because you were going to buy that suit."

"It was on sale, I took it apart and redid it to be exactly what I wanted."

"I thought your clothes were designer. I'm impressed. Why don't you start your own shop?"

"No money."

"We ought to be able to—"

"I don't want a shop. I wouldn't mind selling patterns, but I would be bored to do the same thing over and over . . . and for someone else. I like sewing for myself."

"You're very talented."

"Blessed."

As she looked up at him and smiled, it was he who thought he'd been blessed. And she scared him a little.

About four o'clock, he said, "I need to go by my brother's and check them out to see if he and his family are all behaving. Then I'll go by my place to shower and dress before I come by and pick you up. Okay? Where're we going? Any suggestions?"

"I made reservations at Kaboom's out on St. Joe—"

"Kaboom's? That sounds like noisy fun."

"It is fun. You can wear whatever you like. The food is casual. Sandwiches, snacks."

"Okay. I'll pick you up about six-thirty?"

"What shall I wear?"

"A skirt. I like skirts."

"Well, what will you wear? Jeans? A suit?"

"I'll wear a suit."

"Okay."

Mitch went upstairs and put on the rest of his clothes. When he came down, he grinned at her. Then he held her gently to him. And he kissed her forehead. "I'll be back."

"I'll have to drive you."

"I'd forgotten."

At his apartment he kissed her cheek chastely and got out of the car to watch her drive away. How was he going to order his life so that he could be near to her forever?

After retrieving his car from the parking garage, Mitch went by Rod's. They were out in the yard watching the kids. Mitch sat down, not having even greeted them. He hadn't noticed their greetings, or Pat's sounds of protest as he picked up the kids and hugged their squirmy, wet bodies to his. He didn't mind that the kids were wet.

He sat beside Rod and asked, "Want to sell me your house? You're living over here and it's just empty. It wouldn't have any memories for us."

"Us?"

"Me."

"Pat and I've talked about keeping it for the kids. After they're five, they move over there."

Mitch accepted that idea without comment. "How did you know that Pat was the one?"

"Subconsciously. I never had a choice. It was just predestined. I had to marry Cheryl and Pat had to marry Felix so that we could finally marry. It was fate."

"You just knew?"

"I tried to ignore that fact, but I was caught all along."

"Were you reluctant?"

"Yep. Until the other yahoos began to float around, and I realized I would have to stake my claim."

Mitch nodded. He sat back satisfied and contented. He said, "I'm in love with Sally."

"Really? We'd have never guessed."

"Yeah. I wanted to be sure before I told you."

Rod laughed out loud and looked over at Pat.

Pat said, "Congratulations."

Mitch gave a nod to acknowledge that and said, "I haven't told her yet."

With wonderful irony, Rod said, "She'll be so surprised." Then he laughed again.

"About the house—"

Pat said, "I think Rod should sell it to you. Then he'd be committed."

Rod looked lazily at Pat's rounded stomach and told her, "I'm committed."

"Well, I would like the kids to live with us."

Rod was appalled. "All the time?"

She raised her eyebrows and bobbed her head several times, "Yeah."

"I should have known that ahead of time." He turned to Mitch. "You better start asking Sally questions before you get zonked by her."

Mitch said, "This would be great. I like this garden."

"This is my garden," Pat pointed out. "If you intend sharing it, you have to do half the work."

"The kids have to quit digging it up."

Pat warned, "I don't mind that."

Mitch frowned at her. "God, what a pushover you are."

"I prefer kids to gardens."

"They could play on the driveway or on the sidewalk."

"They can play in the garden."

Mitch looked around, judging, before he said, "Well, you are on a side street. The neighborhood association won't realize what a tacky yard we have."

Pat said, "You can't claim part ownership until you help."

"More kids?"

"More flowers."

"I believe I would enjoy making kids more than digging in gardens."

Rod said with wicked humor, "The kids will help with the digging."

"I've noticed." Mitch looked around then he said, "I've got to meet Sally." That was all. He then simply left.

Rod didn't laugh out loud until Mitch had driven away. His eyes sparkling with his amusement, he turned to Pat. "One thing, when I went with you, I was never that out of it."

"Of course not."

* * *

On his way back to his apartment Mitch discarded his battered box with the leftover condoms and purchased a new box. At his apartment, he removed several from the box and put the box in the drawer of his bedside table.

He showered and dressed, then he took the box from the bedside table and put it under the towels in the linen closet. He put four in his pocket.

He looked around, then left the apartment and drove north to Sally's house. He would see her. They would dance and he would spend most of the evening holding her. Would she go to his place and sleep with him again? He doubted seriously if she would allow him to spend the night with her at her place.

As Sally slowly dressed that evening, she thought about Mitch. What if she did become involved with him? What would that do to her life? If her life was going to go on as she'd planned, now was the time to stop this...madness. It was mad. How could a man affect her this way? He paralyzed her mind and ruined her senses, disrupting her whole system's orderliness.

So...she was attracted physically.

What about her own plans? What if she did take one of the offers she'd received in this past month? Some were very tempting. Expanding. But if she did do that, she would move away from Fort Wayne...and from Mitch.

Would he be convinced to go along so that her career would be advanced as she was capable? Or would he say: Choose.

If he did say that, what would she do? How important was it for her to stretch her limits? She might be able to leave her family and her town, but could she leave Mitch?

He hadn't offered anything. All he'd offered was the desire to be easy together in conversation. That...and just plain, rampant sex. No, it wouldn't be plain or necessarily rampant. He was so sweet and tender... and funny.

She found herself with one stocking on, sitting on the bed, smiling at the wall.

That showed an alarming tendency to distraction. She'd never before had that problem. She was tunnel visioned, dedicated and determined. How could she become so...vapid?

It could just be that he tempted her...sexually. It could just be sex. He was attractive and stirred her senses. That could be all that it was.

She lifted her chin. There was an easy solution. She'd have an affair that could last until she was indifferent and sated, then she would have solved all this distraction.

That was the thing to do.

She finished dressing with eagerness, smiling and humming. She was going to have an affair with Mitchell Goalong. What a name! Just think of being Salamander Goalong! Good gravy!

When Mitch arrived, she was all dressed, made up and perfumed, but not too much. She opened the door and smiled at her victim.

She glowed. He was mesmerized.

They stood and gazed at each other and didn't talk or do anything. Then he said, "Hi."

She smiled wider.

He said, "You're gorgeous."

She said, "This old thing?"

He then noticed her dress. "It's really beautiful...on you."

"You're beautiful, too."

All that seemed like logical conversation to them.

They drove to Kaboom's and it was early for that
place. They found a table and sat down. They ordered wine and smiled at each other. The deejay was
gearing up.

They danced. They almost had the floor to themselves. They checked out the sandwiches and ordered
one that they cut into pieces as a different hors
d'oeuvre.

They had a little more wine and Mitch relaxed. He
had the whole evening. Nobody else was around to
interfere. He could begin his campaign. It didn't matter whose bed they slept in, he was re—

"Well, hel-lo! Fancy meeting you here! It's been
ages!"

Sally got up and hugged the woman. The guy with
the woman kissed Sally's cheek and gave Mitch a smug
look. Mitch got to his feet in a patient, rather territorial way that amused the jeaned-and-plaid-shirted big
guy who wore half boots.

Sally and the other woman were exclaiming and
laughing. The big guy said casually, "I'm Ralph."

Mitch nodded a couple of times. "I'm Mitch."

That appeared to amuse the big guy who was named
Ralph.

Ralph offered no conversation, and Mitch didn't
feel the need to chat, so they stood there.

Sally turned and said, "Betty, this is Mitch Goalong. Mitch, my sister, Betty Travis." As the two in-

troduced ones smiled and said their how-do-you-dos, Sally went on, "And this is Betty's husband, Ralph."

Mitch shook hands with Ralph, considering the jerk hadn't bothered to mention the kinship. Ralph seemed very amused about some damn thing.

"Let's get a bigger table," suggested Betty-the-sister. "Guess who's coming? May and Fred! I thought you'd be surprised. And maybe even Joyce and Tom! How amazing to meet here."

That statement caused trills of laughter. Mitch had never seen Sally so animated.

Ralph indicated another table as if it were his own. And they shifted over there. Mitch felt a decided disappointment. He didn't want to share Sally with anyone else.

Ralph said, "Goalong, that's an interesting name."

And Mitch replied, "Makes you wonder if my ancestor 'went along' with everything, or if the citizens just kept asking him to 'go along' out of there, doesn't it?"

Ralph began to look at Mitch more seriously. He asked with less baiting, "Which do you suppose it was?"

"They were probably inviting him to leave. We aren't particularly leadable."

Ralph's smile was different then. Not less amused but more friendly. "You're dressed up."

"I'm with a classy woman."

"I never thought I'd ever meet a man with a silver tongue. My. You're sharp."

Mitch just watched Ralph with a very faint smile.

Ralph began to make friends. "How about a beer?"

"I've been drinking wine, and if I switch to beer I may be in the floor show."

"They don't have floor shows here."

"They might."

And Ralph laughed a different way, this time with real humor, but he was still amused.

The other predicted people arrived and crowded in. The women were Sally's sisters. The men were the husbands. Mitch knew about big families, having been raised by Salty and Felicia, so he understood the friendship between siblings. He was touched by the sisters' rapport. It was nice to witness.

And he simply got up, went to Sally and took her hand, so that she had to quit talking and get up to dance with him.

She said, "How amazing to run into them all!"

He smiled. He held her. They danced. He saw that they had their table's attention and the three sisters there were talking as they watched their little sister dance with the long, tall stranger.

"Did you tell them you're safe from me for only a day or so?"

"Mitchell!" And she blushed and gasped and laughed.

He grinned down at her and didn't pay any more attention to those waiting at their table. Ralph's table.

Sally saw other people she knew. She would introduce Mitch to them and they would, of course, mention his last name as being odd. Salty told Mitch that people needed things to talk about and not to mind.

He wondered if Sally would mind being Salamander Goalong.

During a slow piece when most of the dancers were using the music as an excuse to just hold each other and talk, Mitch showed Sally off with intricate steps, turns, dips and twirls. He was very good.

Sally laughed and loved it all.

People besides just her family clapped and exclaimed. In those days, not too many men knew how to ballroom dance. When they went back to the table, her sisters clamored to dance. Mitch did hesitate, but since Sally was a skilled dancer he figured her sisters would be able to follow enough.

They were good. Mitch commented, "It's a pleasure to dance with the Yoder women. Not too many women know how to follow."

Betty explained, "With all the kids in our house, we entertained a lot, and the boys and dad cleared out the lower rooms so we could learn to dance and we taught just about everyone out in the county."

"Then you don't live in Fort Wayne?"

"This stifling big city? We're just not city folk."

"Sally is."

"Sally's adaptable. She's special."

Mitch looked down into the bland face of his love's sister and saw the questioning in her eyes, the weighing. He made no comment, but turned Betty carefully in an intricate way that took her mind off questioning or probing while she paid attention to her feet's obedience.

Mitch then looked over toward Sally. There was an older couple at the table and Sally was hugging them. Mitch would bet his new rug that they were The Parents. This was a private screening? Not too subtle.

He took Betty back to the table and, sure enough, he met Sally's parents. He said, "So you're the Salamander's parents."

That surprised them. They gasped and then laughed. His comment threw them off balance completely. Then they looked differently at Sally. More seriously. A little soft. They realized the extent of their daughter's intimacy with this man. She'd told him her real name.

Then they looked at Mitch with some apprehension. Was he a ne'er-do-well wastrel? Could he break her heart?

Back at the table, Mitch said to Joyce, "I have to dance with Sally in between times."

"Tom's going to dance with her."

Mitch smiled a very small smile at Tom and said, "You're next. Right after me." He didn't wait for a reply, but took Sally onto the floor and held her. He said, "I expected to have the whole night holding you. You'll have to come to my place and placate my ego."

"I've never seen an ego less in need of placating. You're sassy and I haven't had but two dances."

"Your sisters are nice women. Your parents would love Salty and Felicia. Our families would meld perfectly. Do you believe we could endure each other, so that all those people could have that excellent relationship?"

"You're serious?"

He groaned against her cheek. "Killingly."

"That's sex."

"That is included."

She warned, "Our lives would change."

"Yeah."

"What if I was fired and had to leave town?"

He shrugged. "I'm movable."

"A man's job comes first generally. How would you feel if I felt my own job came first with me?"

"We could commute."

She rejected that. "No. I would want to sleep with you."

"You've just admitted that I'd come first with you."

"Did I?"

He danced her backward, brushing against her, holding her. "You sure 'nuff did."

"I'll be darned."

"Do you love me?"

She looked up at him so vulnerably. "Something's sure going on. You...unsettle me. I—"

"You...what?"

She obviously switched subjects. "If you should marry me, you would know all the family's real names. It might frighten you."

"And your great-grandmother is still alive?"

"She's almost a hundred years old."

"I believe I shall have it in our marriage agreement that Salty and Felicia get to name any of the kids. Would that block your great-granny?"

"You'd have to do the negotiating."

"When can we go see her?"

"Not tonight."

"Tomorrow's Sunday. How about then?"

She laughed.

"We have to get everything cleared up ahead of time. It would save a lot of arguments and slammed doors and crocodile tears."

"I don't use tears as a weapon. I have more pride than that."

"Good."

When the lovers finally left Kaboom's, saying and calling goodbyes to her family and friends, the silence inside his car was—intimate. Sally became intensely aware of him, of his breathing, of his being a person she cared about.

She said, "Let's go to your place."

Her words jolted through him so that he braked the car on the empty street and turned toward her to be sure it was she who had spoken and not his libido.

Her eyes widened. "You are shocked?"

"Do you mean it?"

"Well, you spent the afternoon in my bed," she explained demurely, tilting her head several times. She licked her lips in a quick, nervous flick and continued, "So it seems only right that I have a turn...in yours."

"Yes." The simple reply, to indicate he agreed, was hoarse. A little boggled, he stared and finally realized they were stopped in the middle of the street. He took his foot off the brake and touched the gas pedal. He drove downtown silently. He didn't want to say anything that might change her mind.

He parked his car in the parking garage and he handled her exiting the car as if she were fragile glass. He escorted her to his apartment, still silent, but excessively attentive and breathing in a broken way.

She was not calm, but she strived to appear so.

When they went into his bedroom, he said, "Are you sure?"

She just nodded in a tremor and glanced his way a couple of times in the series of glances she managed, but she didn't really see anything. She didn't know what to do next.

He said, "Let me take off your clothes."

"I can do that."

"I'd like the privilege."

"I think . . . it would embarrass me terribly."

"Please."

"Maybe another time."

"Do you want to go into the bathroom? Or do you want me to go into the living room while you get into bed?"

"Yes."

He waited to see which she wanted, and since she didn't move he went into the bathroom. When he opened the door again, the bedroom was dark and she was in his bed. He shivered and sweated and his hands trembled. It was just a good thing he was then prepared for her.

He eased carefully into bed, under the sheet and moved near her. His breathing was chuffing and he felt like an animal. Surely he could handle this situation with some finesse?

She said, "I finished my period three days ago. I needed more time."

"I understand. Are you sure now?"

"Uh-hmm."

"Oh, Salamander!" And air whooshed out of his lungs and he trembled as he carefully took her against him. "I'm going to kiss you," he warned.

"I'm braced."

But it was just like always. Chaos.

And their mating was just as cosmic. Their bodies twisted and strained and moved with the planets. It was awesome. And the debris of what was left of them fell finally back onto his bed.

They were inert. Their subconsciouses struggled to get their life-support systems back into some semblance of efficiency. It took a while.

In the darkness, his voice was husky. "Your body is beautiful."

"So's yours."

"You are wondrous."

"So are you."

And they slept without moving again.

Ten

It was really very early when Mitchell Goalong and Sally Yoder wakened to find each other nearby. They smiled and smiled and then laughed. They got up and went to the bathroom and got a drink of water and stood around looking at each other in the dim light of a beginning dawn.

Their eyes were tender and their smiles were mushy. Their touches were gentle as they stood apart. But that didn't last long. They went back to bed and participated in the whole amazing emotional clash yet again.

But they took a little longer. Long enough to smooth their hands on one another and explore a bit. Not much, but a beginning of appreciation. And their coupling was gentle and slow at first. They tried very hard to keep an even pace, to show a little restraint. Foolish, foolish couple. The whole episode dissolved into a flaming nova.

So they slept again.

Boneless and witless, they arrived at the lake only a couple of hours late. They hunted down Pike and his buddies and gave no reason for their delayed arrival.

They sat smiling and listless, participating enough by listening to the more active people as they swam off the pontoon boat and barbecued just about everything including the pineapple chunks. The two lovers exchanged glances and smiled. It was as if they'd come down from Mount Olympus to observe human behavior in an indulgent manner.

And with the late afternoon, Mitch announced their departure and the two left to go back to his apartment. But along the way, Sally said, "It's my house's turn. We need to go there."

So they had to stop and buy another box of condoms.

It's one thing to make love in the dark, but to do it in broad summer light is revealing, and Sally was one continuous, complete blush.

Mitchell was charmed. He smiled and smiled and smiled. He lay her down on her bed and watched his hand on her.

She watched his face.

He knew that and would look up at her and smile yet more. Then he kissed her here and there. He nuzzled and pushed his face against her slowly, relishing the feel of her.

She sighed and began to move and to turn a little so that he would touch where she wanted. It was a slow, beautiful, supine dance of love. The movements were exquisite and languorous . . . at first.

But their breaths picked up, their eyes closed slowly as their lips parted. And damned if they didn't get to kissing and that shot them right off into space again.

Their hands became tense and greedy and their bodies were demanding and their minds buzzed with satisfying their needs. They turned and pressed and wiggled and stroked, breathing fire and feeling its liquid rushing in their veins. All was chaos yet again!

And again they survived.

When they could speak, at last, in that sweat-soaked, rumpled bed, Mitch commented, "Humans must be pretty sturdy, if all sexual encounters are anything like it is with us."

"I've wondered about that since last night." Sally's fingers turned his sweat-dampened hair into ringlets. "I've never heard anyone mention any surprise at what happens when they've made love. Do you suppose it's like this for everyone? And they just accept it as being natural?"

He shook his head minimally. "I don't know."

"It's stunning."

"Yes."

"I'm surprised we survive," she commented idly.

"Yeah."

"Just the lack of oxygen out there."

So she, too, knew they left the planet each time.

They looked at each other. She said, "This is serious."

"Yes."

And they were silent as they studied each other, understanding the ramifications of their encounter. It was, indeed, serious.

So that week hurried by in something of a blur. On the next Sunday, Mitchell and Sally went to the Home to visit her great-granny. With some discomfort, Sally warned Mitch, "She's quite old, you must remember. Mother says she was such a fragile and particular lady, but now she belches quite loudly. I don't want you to be embarrassed."

"I won't. What's her name?"

"Susan Yoder."

"Why does she have such a simple name, when she names all the kids such complicated ones?"

"I have no idea."

They had to wait while the attendants got Mrs. Yoder up and into her chair and wheeled her out to the visiting room saying loudly, "You have company! Isn't that nice?"

Sally told Mitch, "With all of us around here, she has someone visiting her every day."

The old lady was tiny in her wheelchair. She had a belt around her that held her up and to the back of the chair. She looked transparent.

She said in a loud voice, "So you're Salamander's beau."

He said, "Yes, ma'am."

She grinned.

Mitch said, "I'll bet you were a handful in your young days, a lady like you."

She lifted her chin just exactly the way Sally lifted hers. "I don't remember being a lady. I'm not even sure I'm still female. The last orderly I propositioned was shocked. He said he was young enough to be my grandson. I thought he was bragging." She lifted a clawed hand up to tuck in a wisp of her hair which had been dyed red.

"My husband once threatened to horsewhip me. I went out to the barn and got the whip and hit him with it."

Sally was shocked. "No! Great-granny, you didn't!"

"No man ever threatened me and got away with it. You remember that. This one looks like he'd want to be boss and he'll be so sweet about it so that you won't notice. You pay attention."

"Yes ma'am."

Mitch put in, "Hush, Susan Yoder. Quit giving this sweet girl your wicked advice."

"See? I knew it. Just look at him!" And Great-granny Yoder laughed and shifted her teeth.

Mitch guessed shrewdly, "I'll bet you've tried just about everything. You're lucky your generation isn't around to tattle on you. Did you ever chew tobacco?"

"I did try. Benjamin had a fit."

Sally said, "Benjamin was her husband."

"You must have worn him out."

Her face sobered. "He told me he'd wait for me this side of the River Styx. I'm counting on it. I don't know why it's taking me so long."

Mitch said softly, "Maybe it's so you can name our babies."

Sally gave him an appalled glance, but he was watching Susan.

"So you're planning on that, are you? What's Salamander say about you?"

"She may like me...enough."

Susan Yoder gave him a clear, pale-eyed look and smiled. "Bet you a nickel."

"I'm on your side."

"She's going to have her work cut out for her, trying to keep you in line."

And Mitch said gently, "I'll help her."

"Yep. That'd be the way he'll do it, Salamander. He'll be so crafty and slick, you'll only think you have control."

After they said goodbye and left, Sally said in shock to Mitch, "You *invited* her to name the kids! How could you do that?"

"They'll have memorable names. She didn't like being called Susan. She must have had an enemy named Susan."

"I'll ask my grandmother."

He looked at Sally. "I'll bet you a nickel."

She smiled. "That Susan Yoder has been a handful all her life. Mother almost ran away from home when she lived with us."

"What'd your dad do?"

"He talked to his dad, her son."

"What'd he do?"

"He said, 'Good luck.' "

Mitch laughed.

Sally complained, "How *could* you give her permission to name our babies?"

"Then you do admit that you'll share babies with me?"

"Probably."

"You have to marry me first."

"Yeah."

"You don't sound melting and loving and wishy-washy."

"I can't believe you'd do a thing like that to our little unborn babies! They have no say-so at all!"

"They'll find the names different and be smug about them."

She looked at her love and to her irritation she thought he might be right. Nobody else had ever asked Susan if she'd ever chewed tobacco. Mitchell Goalong was not a conformist or ordinary. He didn't mind having Goalong for a name. His children would be just as peculiar. Just watch.

In that next week they went to work and performed very well. They didn't seek each other's company, in order to conceal the fact that they were lovers. But they fooled no one.

They would exchange a glance across the store and everyone who was unfortunate enough to be standing between the two felt like a plucked chicken that had just been singed in a fire.

And the next weekend Mitch took Sally to meet his foster parents and his old aunt.

The aunt wasn't as old as Sally's great-grandmother, Susan Yoder, but she was close. Great-aunt Maddie still lived on her own, with a wonderful support group who took her shopping and cooked and cleaned for her and saw to it that she was comfortable.

Great-aunt Maddie was charming to Sally. And Sally was bright enough to have a tape recorder as the old aunt told about Mitchell's family. Unfortunately, the Goalong women had all been put-upon and the men had all been scoundrels.

Off to one side, out of Great-aunt Maddie's vision, Mitchell shook his head in denial, but his eyes sparkled with his humor.

And at Temple, Ohio, the Brown household was very close to being like the Yoders' over in Indiana.

The only difference was that the Yoders were all actual kin.

Sally told Felicia, "I'm glad Mitch had you to help him as a child."

"He was interesting. Very competitive, an organizer. He could argue on anything. We miss him." Felicia's big, dramatic eyes really saw Sally, and her wonderful voice was soft and gentle with this woman who loved Mitchell Goalong. "We're so glad Mitch found you."

With a feeling of having cleared all the hurdles, the two lovers returned to Fort Wayne. Everything appeared to go well. The lovers were discreet, at least in their own eyes, and life was wonderful.

However, it was just a couple of weeks later at the beginning of September, that Mitchell happened to learn that Sally had another project brewing. It wasn't tape ratings or advertisements or sly enticements for customers, it was the female Jamison named Abigail. She was a Jamison and she was female.

Mitch asked that Busy Bee, Sally Yoder, his love, his life, and all that stuff, but he asked with patient logic and a great deal of suspicion, "Why are you encouraging Abigail Jamison to wear gray suits during the days—just like her male relatives?"

And Sally Yoder replied with equal logic, "She's a Jamison."

"So?"

Sally replied the obvious, "Although female, she is qualified to take her place in the Jamison hierarchy."

"There must be a taint in your genes you've failed to mention. What are you hiding from me?"

She finished refolding a blouse, precisely, and lifted her eyebrows in a kind way, being surprised he hadn't grasped basics. "She has a master's in business from Yale."

"You're the woman who was offered a cigar by the Jamisons. They aren't really aware of women being in business."

"Then it's time they learned."

So Mitch spent some time looking out his door at Rembrandt's windmill, which hung on the wall across from his door. The lowering skies seemed appropriate. A storm was building in Jamisons. His Busy Bee was poking her nose into something else that was none of her business.

In the days that followed, Mitch read with greater interest the job openings in the *Wall Street Journal*.

When the two were alone and with an unslakable hunger, he made COSMIC love to Sally, risking their brain cells carelessly in the wild tumultuous clashings of their souls' need. And when he could speak, he assured her, "I'll take care of you."

Her fuzzy brain did hear that and register it. She asked, "Hmmm?"

"You don't have to worry about anything. No matter what happens, I'll take care of you."

It was an impressive struggle, in her condition, but she did surface, and asked, "What are you talking about?"

"That I love you. I want to marry you. And I'll always take care of you, no matter what happens."

She looked at him clear-eyed and attentive. "Am I being fired again?"

"No."

"Then what put you on this caretaking binge?"

"I want you to feel secure."

"I am secure."

"I want you to know I'll take care of you."

He'd said it yet again. Sally replied, "That's very nice of you. I'll take care of you, too, but evenly. Not too much, not too little."

"Thank you."

"What brought on this conversation?"

"I love you."

She smiled. "Are you feeling macho and caveman-ish?"

"Not right this minute."

"How could you have come out of that tailspin we were in and get so practical and logical? I feel as if I have the bends for making too quick a trip back from wherever it is that you insist on taking me to—end-lessly!"

"It isn't endless—"

"Don't get vulgar."

"Are you going to marry me?" he asked carefully.

"Probably."

"I need the security of having my name branded on—"

"What did you say?" she inquired, and even put a hand to cup her ear.

"Uh... Give me a minute. I'll figure a different way of saying it."

"Was Great-granny right in her snap analysis of you being a dominant male?"

"No."

She turned her head on the pillow and looked off as she tightened the sides of her mouth in disgust. "That's a 101 basic dominate male reply! Good grief. Couldn't you have soothed me and convinced me that you will allow me to rule?"

"I'm depleted right now. Wait a bit and I'll work on that."

"See? There you go again. You're supposed to get on your knees and beg my forgiveness."

"Why?"

"For acting as if you're equal."

He nodded soberly, but his eyes sparkled and he had to lick his lips. He lay back flat and put one forearm over his eyes as he said, "I have a headache."

"You do?" She curled up anxiously and leaned over, looking at him as she lay her hand on his forehead.

But he laughed.

She straightened up and gasped. "Are you manipulating me?"

"Not right now. I'm drained."

"You wicked, wicked man!" She attacked him, trying to push him off the bed. They wrestled, and she squealed, and he laughed.

And he'd lied about being drained.

Probably the culmination was the yearly banquet in which people were retired and recognized and praised. It was held at the Grand Wayne Center and it was posh. The store's suppliers were invited to contribute to the doings and to attend, and everyone dressed up and made an Event of it.

The news media had been reminded of the date and the tables were set up perfectly. Edgar and his two nephews would be at the head table.

Mitch looked at the seating arrangement and saw that Abigail was seated at one of the round tables just below the head table.

He went over to the Wayne Center to be sure everything was going well and he saw Sally. She really had no official business there and he just watched. She was sitting at a round table in front of the head table. It took a bit for Mitch to recognize that Sally was being tested for the lighting.

Mitch thought how much time and thought she gave to the Jamisons store. She was an employee that anyone would treasure. He felt mellow, smiling a little, watching his love.

She went to his apartment with him and they dressed for the occasion. He loved putting his gift of a diamond drop pendant around her throat. He kissed her shoulder and told her, "You'll be the most beautiful woman there."

"Nonsense."

"I've watched at all the gatherings we've shared from the very beginning and I can tell you truthfully that you're the most beautiful woman in all the country."

"You've not been up in the far northwest. There could be a woman up there who is more beautiful."

"*People* magazine would have had her picture on their cover. They have not. They are still looking for you. No other woman would have received all the mail you did after that brief appearance on World News Network."

She put the back of her hand to her forehead, then checked the hand to see if the fingers were curled right and put it back. "It's a burden."

"You're just lucky we're both dressed and have to be there in fifteen minutes... Hey, fifteen minutes should do it. Hold still! No! Quit resisting. I won't smear your makeup. You don't even have to lie down.

I'll put you against the wall. Sally, you're the most selfish—beautiful woman I've ever known!''

"You've used this whole snow job on other women?''

"No.''

So it wasn't until they arrived at the center that Mitch saw Abigail had arrived wearing a female version of the Jamison tuxedo. Mitch instantly assimilated the fact that Sally had rigged a light to beam down on Abigail as she sat in front of the head table.

Mitch felt a slow chill run up his skin. He knew that Sally had contrived that outfit for Abigail. She was using her manipulations to pry Abigail right into the Jamisons trio. Sally was pushing. Again.

Abigail was serene. She smiled and was courteously friendly. But Mitch saw her wink at Sally. They were in collusion! What had Sally begun? How was he to get her out of this mess?

Mitch considered the ramifications of defending the Busy Bee. Then he looked over at his love. They'd go to California and ride the waves when the state broke away from the continent. She was worthy of a new country, independent of the mainland. He would help stabilize the new California Island's economy and take a hand in fair trade with the depleted area of the United States.

Having decided on the outcome of the explosive evening, Mitchell Goalong found his love and seated her beside him. They had no hand in the ceremonies or in the presentations and could simply be onlookers.

As the speeches droned along, Mitch saw as the Jamisons noted their niece and gradually became aware of her solitary spotlight. They put an elbow on the table and thoughtfully rubbed their chins. One nephew used the wrong elbow.

Mitch looked at Abigail. She was courteously concentrated on the speaker, one elbow—the correct one—was on the table. She was thoughtfully rubbing her chin.

People are not stupid. The employees at Jamisons had watched as Sally had coached Abigail and dressed her to match her uncles and grandfather. They were amused and excited with the byplay and very interested.

And the master of ceremonies, reading along, introduced Abigail Jamison as a new employee!

Edgar looked at the emcee in some surprise. But Abigail stood and bowed from the hips in a lovely version of the male bow. Everyone applauded.

And then Sally rose, applauding.

Mitch couldn't allow her to stand alone, so he also stood up and applauded.

So everyone else stood, and finally so did Edgar and his two nephews. It had been Sally who'd triggered it. It takes only a couple of standing ones to start the reaction. Ahhh, calculation.

Nothing else untoward happened. The people mixed and Mitch slitted his eyes as the two culprits met with cordial formality, nodding their heads like pros. They were.

Mitch took that Busy Bee home to his apartment. And he waited until he was inside with the door closed before he said, "You testing the waters?"

She looked like an innocent, unknowing woman. She blinked as if she was puzzling out his opening sentence and smiled just a little. "Testing?"

"Maybe I should have said, Stretching. How far do you think you can go this time?"

She shrugged indifferently and replied, "We'll see."

He went to his closet and searched, then to the bureau and searched some more, then to the spare room and found what he wanted. It was a red shirt. "Here. This is for you to wear. I don't have a red cape."

Was she intimidated? No. She smiled as she took the shirt. "Thank you."

When she was so relaxed that sleep was necessary, Mitch lay awake and plotted and planned. He'd say, "We really want a wider choice." He'd say, "If she goes, I go." He'd say, "You're making the mistake of your life." He'd say, "Who needs this anarchy?"

And his dreams were of turbulence.

Their weekend was one of busyness. They were with her family twice, once for a meal, and Mitch watched them and listened. They were really fine people. Their children would have good kinsmen to back them. Too bad they wouldn't be living close.

He watched the Busy Bee interfering and giving advice and being contradicted and adjusting to that. And he knew she was so special that he could never find anyone else even close to her perfection. She was, indeed, perfect.

They met with friends of hers and then with friends he was making. And he liked all those people.

And they went to see Rod and Pat. Privately, Mitch told Rod, "There's a big blowup coming at Jamisons. Sally is right in the middle of it, as usual, and it could well be that we won't be here to live next door to you."

Rod lazily replied, "It'll work out. You can always do brakes down at the shop."

Mitch laughed.

Sunday night Sally went to her own place to spend the night. "I need to do some washing and I need to iron some blouses for this next week."

"You ought to move in with me."

"I will. But not until after we're married."

"I love you, Salamander."

"I know." She smiled at him for a serious minute, then she said gently, "You have to realize that I could be fired tomorrow?"

"I believe they're smarter than that."

"But you do recognize the possibility?"

"No."

She laughed. "You're a wonderful man. You're so unpredictable. My mind's been thinking of all the ways the Jamisons could react to this outrageous push for Abigail. She and I will probably both be on the carpet tomorrow. Introducing her in that spotlight was chancy."

"No," said Mitch seriously. "It was the proper thing for *them* to have done."

"But not us."

"It was pushy. And those Jamisons aren't necessarily pushable."

"But don't you think it will be interesting to see how they will handle it?"

"You know I back you."

"I'm on my own in this. I will not involve you."

"I am involved."

"That's personal. This is business. Don't get the two confused."

He smiled at her in some pride. ''You're a strong woman.''

''Yep. So's Abigail.''

''I'll be around tomorrow.''

''I love you, Mitch.''

''I'm partial to you.''

''Don't kiss me.''

He'd frowned and mentioned, ''You'd think we could get a little used to this kissing. Why does it always happen that way?''

''We're ordained to be mated.''

''Okay.''

''Not right now.''

Since she was adamant, Mitch walked her down to her car and watched her drive away. She wasn't zonked. She drove airily. He hadn't kissed her just before she left. He'd just kissed her hand.

He stood on the curb, watching her drive away and wondered if they would ever be able to kiss casually. Other people could. Why couldn't they? Would he be able to kiss her at the altar when they were married? Discreetly kiss her? Chastely?

He sighed, put his hands into his pockets and went back to his apartment. He went to his desk and opened his personal Jamisons address book. Then he dialed a number and talked. He mentioned that the great majority of shoppers at Jamisons were women.

So on Monday, when Sally got to work, there was a note that a staff meeting would be held at ten o'clock.

Abigail came by Sally's cubbyhole and said, ''Courage.''

Sally replied, ''To hell with them all.''

Abigail drew herself up in mock horror and asked, "My sweet granddaddy and my devoted uncles?"

And Sally replied, "Yeah."

Abigail raised an imaginary glass. "To progress!"

"To women," Sally amended.

And Mitch came slowly along, his hands in his pockets. "Is this a feminists' meeting?"

"We welcome men to see the light."

He said with a warning, "We may see it."

"I told you. Don't get yourself involved. You're too valuable to this organization. Too many people would have it tougher just because the Jamisons are not really in touch with progress. Sorry, Abigail—"

"But what you say is true."

"Yes. But Mitch is needed here more than we are."

"Well..." Abigail smiled at Mitch with sparkling eyes of humor. "When I make it to the top, wherever, I'll want to hire him."

Sally said loftily, "I'll consider it."

"I said 'him,' not you."

"I know. I help him negotiate."

Mitch put in, "I handle my own jobs."

"See?" Abigail said to Sally. "He's just stubborn."

Sally said, "I believe he can be influenced."

Mitch nodded soberly in agreement. "Well, it's about time. Let's go see what happens."

The Jamisons made Abigail a junior vice president.

There was a silence, then Sally and Abigail began to laugh. Edgar passed around cigars, but excused the ladies from accepting them.

Sally turned and her look met Mitch's eyes. She gave him a narrow-eyed evaluation and pushed her lower lip up as she nodded minutely as if agreeing with herself.

And Mitch knew she suspected his hand in the arrangement. He would never confirm it.

When she cornered him at lunch, she asked, "How did you manage that?"

"What?"

"You know."

"No." Mitch appeared as if innocent.

"Why did the Jamisons make Abigail a junior vice president?"

"Well, I suppose that if they'd made her a senior vice president so soon after her leaving school someone in the family would raise hell?"

"Can you out-and-out deny that you didn't finagle this?"

"They wouldn't dare to fire you, with Abigail a VP. It would look tacky."

"You're avoiding a reply."

"Do I look like a man who has influence?"

"Yes. A sneaky, crafty creature, just like all other men."

"Why, Salamander Yoder, how could you be that sexist? We need to work on your attitude."

"How do you intend to do that?"

They were married on October 10. It had to be a large wedding, with all the kin and ramifications of family they both had. Great-granny Susan attended with attendants, and she laughed when Mitch barely kissed Sally's forehead after the ceremony.

And after that, in the rest of their long lives together, Sally and Mitch never did kiss in public. Their cosmic tilting kisses never diminished. And like Rod and Pat, and all the rest, they too lived happily ever after.

Weeelll . . . most of the time.

* * * * *

A romantic collection that
will touch your heart....

to
Mother
with
Love
'93

Diana Palmer
Debbie Macomber
Judith Duncan

As part of your annual tribute to
motherhood, join three of Silhouette's
best-loved authors as they celebrate the
joy of one of our most precious gifts—
mothers.

Available in May at your favorite retail outlet.

Only from 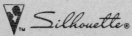 *Silhouette*®

—where passion lives.

INTIMATE MOMENTS®

10TH
Anniversary

Celebrate our anniversary with a fabulous collection of firsts....

The first Intimate Moments titles written by three of your favorite authors:

NIGHT MOVES   Heather Graham Pozzessere
LADY OF THE NIGHT   Emilie Richards
A STRANGER'S SMILE   Kathleen Korbel

Silhouette Intimate Moments is proud to present a FREE hardbound collection of our authors' firsts—titles that you will treasure in the years to come from some of the line's founding members.

This collection will not be sold in retail stores and is available only through this exclusive offer. Look for details in Silhouette Intimate Moments titles available in retail stores in May, June and July.

SIMANN

SILHOUETTE® Desire®

MAN OF THE MONTH: 1993

**They're tough, they're sexy...
and they know how to get the
job done....
Caution: They're**

MEN AT WORK

Blue collar... white collar ... these men are working overtime
to earn your love.

January:	Businessman Lyon Cantrell in Joan Hohl's LYON'S CUB
February:	Landscaper-turned-child-saver David Coronado in Raye Morgan's THE BACHELOR
March:	Woodworker Will Lang in Jackie Merritt's TENNESSEE WALTZ
April:	Contractor Jake Hatcher in Dixie Browning's HAZARDS OF THE HEART (her 50th Silhouette Book)
May:	Workaholic Cooper Maitland in Jennifer Greene's QUICKSAND
June:	Wheeler-dealer Tyler Tremaine in Barbara Boswell's TRIPLE TREAT

And that's just your first six months' pay! Let these men make
a direct deposit into your heart. MEN AT WORK... only from
Silhouette Desire!

MOM93JJ

For all those readers who've been looking for something a little bit different, a little bit spooky, let Silhouette Books take you on a journey to the dark side of love with

SILHOUETTE Shadows™

If you like your romance mixed with a hint of danger, a taste of something eerie and wild, you'll love Shadows. This new line will send a shiver down your spine and make your heart beat faster. It's full of romance and more—and some of your favorite authors will be featured right from the start. Look for our four launch titles wherever books are sold, because you won't want to miss a single one.

THE LAST CAVALIER—Heather Graham Pozzessere
WHO IS DEBORAH?—Elise Title
STRANGER IN THE MIST—Lee Karr
SWAMP SECRETS—Carla Cassidy

After that, look for two books every month, and prepare to tremble with fear—and passion.

SILHOUETTE SHADOWS, coming your way in March.

Silhouette®

SHAD1

SILHOUETTE® Desire®

HAWK'S WAY

HAWK'S WAY—where the Whitelaws of Texas run free till passion brands their hearts. A hot new series from Joan Johnston!

Look for the first of a long line of Texan adventures, beginning in April with THE RANCHER AND THE RUNAWAY BRIDE (D #779), as Tate Whitelaw battles her bossy brothers—and a sexy rancher.

Next, in May, Faron Whitelaw meets his match in THE COWBOY AND THE PRINCESS (D #785).

Finally, in June, Garth Whitelaw shows you just how hot the summer can get in THE WRANGLER AND THE RICH GIRL (D #791).

Join the Whitelaws as they saunter about HAWK'S WAY looking for their perfect mates . . . only from Silhouette Desire!